Erin Soderberg (Downing) has written many books for children and young adults, but this is her first 7–9 series. Before beginning to write full time, Erin worked as a children's book editor and marketer, spent a few months as a biscuit inventor and also worked for Nickelodeon. She lives in Minneapolis, Minnesota, with her delightfully quirky family.

The Quirks
Welcome to Normal

Erin Soderberg

Illustrated by Kelly Light

BLOOMSBURY

LONDON NEW DELHI NEW YORK SYDNEY

Bloomsbury Publishing, London, New Delhi, New York and Sydney

First published in Great Britain in July 2013 by Bloomsbury Publishing Plc
50 Bedford Square, London WC1B 3DP

A CIP catalogue record for this book is available from the British Library

ISBN 978 1 4088 4171 6

1 3 5 7 9 10 8 6 4 2

Printed and bound in Great Britain by CPI Group (UK) Ltd, Croydon CR0 4YY

www.bloomsbury.com

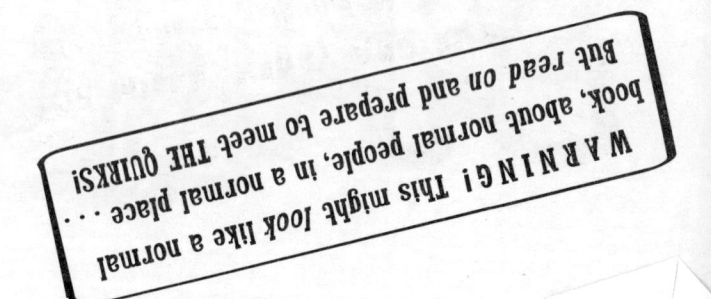

WARNING! This might look like a normal
book, about normal people, in a normal place
. . . But read on and prepare to meet THE QUIRKS!

FOR MILLA, HENRY AND RUBY

Who inspire me with their clever ideas
and boundless imagination
(And also give me all the hugs I need)

Table of Contents

CHAPTER 1

The Fifth House on the Left

Not so very long ago, there was a house in Normal, Michigan, where nothing was as it seemed. If you happened to stroll by on a warm September afternoon, you might have thought the house was perfectly plain and comfortably normal. Just a white clapboard house surrounded by other white clapboard houses, sixteen to a block. But if you were the rare sort of person who *notices* things, you might have spotted the differences.

The thorny roses that climbed up the

crumbling steps of this particular house were always wilted. That itself was troubling enough for a pleasant neighbourhood. But some days, the flowers were a different colour than they were the day before. These roses had a tendency to change colour with the weather and with one young girl's mood.

A white picket fence that ought to have matched all the others in the neighbourhood instead had a pinkish tint. For several weeks, it smelled faintly of ham and pickle sandwiches.

And if you looked very, very closely, you might have seen a tiny fairy grandmother darting between the drooping branches of the willow tree.

Luckily, no one ever took the time to look closely. And *that* was a very good thing.

Because when the front gate closed behind the

people who lived in that house, almost everything ordinary was left on the other side of the ham-scented fence. Inside, the Quirk family was anything but normal – it was just that no one in Normal had noticed.

At least, not yet.

CHAPTER 2

Penelope Quirk's
Strange-Mazing Imagination

"Hold still, Molly. I need to focus." Penelope Quirk jabbed one long finger at her twin sister, threatening to tickle her if she didn't stop squirming. "I'm going to try to make you blonde." Penelope giggled.

"OK." Molly Quirk shrugged, laughing a nearly identical laugh. "I like blonde hair. Then people won't get us mixed up!" Molly wiggled her toes and closed her eyes, relaxing in the privacy of her family's garden deck.

Penelope – who was often called Pen – automatically matched her sister's movements. Both Quirk girls stretched out, belly up, on the wooden deck. Molly snuck a peek at her sister and whispered, "But after this you should rest, Pen. Remember, school starts tomorrow." Molly lay back, letting her dark-brown spiral curls rest comfortably on a half-flat helium balloon.

The "Welcome to Normal" balloon was one of several dozen identical balloons that had been delivered by neighbours when the Quirk family moved into their house a few days earlier. No one had brought over muffins or carrot cake or even lasagne. Instead, the Quirks had a collection of twenty-six floppy silver balls that no one was willing to pop and throw out.

In the few days since they'd arrived in their new town, Molly and Penelope had noticed that almost everyone in Normal enjoyed doing everything the same as their neighbours. They all planted the same flowers, lined up in tidy rows, in front of their houses. The men in town had the same haircut, parted neatly on the left. And at

6

least half the families drove either a tan or blue people carrier. The Quirks' new town was pleasant and perfect.

Molly shivered on the back deck, despite the warm afternoon sun. She squinted at her sister and said, "OK, I'm sort of chickening out. What if this actually works? Mum will freak."

"It's not going to work," Penelope muttered, rolling over and pursing her lips. She was trying hard to concentrate, but something deep down inside her was making it difficult to focus. Perhaps it was because Pen *liked* that she and Molly looked exactly the same. "Controlling my magic never works. But just hush, so I can at least try."

The Quirk girls had been in the garden for almost two hours, frittering away their last summer afternoon before the first day of fourth grade. As she had done every year on the day before school began, Pen was preparing. She was trying to boss around her imagination.

Like other almost-fourth graders, Penelope Quirk had a vivid and wild imagination, full of fantasy and fun and silliness. But unlike other almost–fourth graders, Penelope Quirk's imagination had a tendency to roar into life – literally.

Most people have a filter – a little switch in their heads that keeps them from saying and doing the strange or rude or just-plain-wrong things that pop into their minds all day long. But Penelope's switch didn't work as it should. Penelope could keep her mouth from saying it, but her mind was a different matter.

When Pen was nervous or distracted (or sometimes when she had to go to the bathroom in that way that made her cross her legs and turn yellow), Penelope lost control of her thoughts and *poof!* the tucked-away corners of her imagination became real, just like that.

For the last few years, Penelope even had an honest-to-goodness monster living under her bed. Molly had named their monster Niblet, because of his super-teensy toes. Niblet was the only thing Penelope's imagination had *poofed!* into existence that hadn't disappeared within a few minutes. No one could figure out why the big guy had stuck around, but he was a welcome part of the family now.

"OK, here goes." Penelope squeezed her eyes closed and bunched up her lips, making her concentration face. She let an image of a blonde Molly drift through her mind and momentarily cracked up. Pen hummed, trying to focus every last bit of attention on Molly's curls going golden.

Suddenly, a plane roared overhead. Penelope watched as it left a wispy white trail of steam in its wake. As hard as it was for her not to follow the aeroplane's path through the sky as it soared off to wherever, Penelope closed her eyes again before the vapour trail melted away. "Anything yet?" she squeaked, peeking at her sister, who was still stretched out beside her.

Molly lifted her head and shook her twisty curls in the thick, humid air. Still brown. "Nope. Keep trying."

"This is useless," Pen moaned. She sat up and picked absent-mindedly at a blob of mustard that had been stuck to her shorts since lunchtime. "Why can't I make stuff appear or change when I want it to? Everything just *happens* when I *don't* want it to," Pen grumbled. Molly couldn't help but laugh a little at her twin sister's sour face.

But Molly stopped laughing when angry steam started to billow out of Penelope's ears. The steam smelled like cabbage soup, which smelled like stinky feet. It smelled so bad that Molly sat up straight, tucked her nose inside the top of her shirt, and squeezed. Molly put a comforting hand over her sister's and gave it a little hand hug. "We'll figure out how to control your Quirk one of these days. I promise," she said from inside her shirt.

"Will I figure it out before we have to move again?" Penelope asked, lifting an eyebrow. (Brow-lifting was a trick both girls had been working on for several years, and, unlike her magic, it was something Penelope had mastered.) Molly didn't say anything, so Pen answered her own question. "Probably not. Normal seems perfect, so I'm sure we won't get to stay. We're not going to fit in here any better than we have anywhere else."

Penelope knew that she had really messed things up for the Quirks in quite a few towns – from Springfield to Hackensack to Pawtucket to Sandstone. The Quirks had lived in twelve states and twenty-six towns in the nine (and three-quarter) years Molly and Penelope had been alive. In that time, far too many people had witnessed the Quirks' special brand of magic.

As the girls stared up at the clouds, a herd of thundering cloud elephants suddenly came to life in the sky above them and stampeded across the smooth, baby-blue background. Gloomy storm clouds formed under each elephant stomp and made the sky messy and black.

"Clouds, clouds, normal clouds . . ." Penelope said, squeezing her eyes closed tight. Her body tensed with the effort of trying to control her thoughts.

Molly began to whistle a Beatles song. As she did, she wished – not for the first time – that there were something more she could do. But there wasn't. She was as plain as Penelope was colourful. Molly was magic-less, like a big bowl of boring vanilla ice cream in a family full of wacky flavours.

Penelope's face relaxed as she sang along with her sister. Then, as quickly as they'd come, the elephants melted back into puffy-fluffy clouds and drifted calmly across the sky again.

Next door, the girls could see their unfriendly neighbour, Mrs DeVille, closing and opening her windows angrily as she watched the storm come, then just as quickly go. Pen and Molly looked at each other and grinned. Things were looking clear in Normal. For now.

CHAPTER 3

Grandpa Quill and His Rewinding Eggs

When Molly skipped into the kitchen the next morning, on her first day of fourth grade, the table was a mess. It looked like someone's pockets had thrown up on the speckled green surface. It was covered in papers and wrappers and crumpled dollar bills from the tip jar at the restaurant where Molly's mum, Bree, worked as a waitress.

Molly and Penelope had both flung their jumpers over the back of a kitchen chair the night before. Their little brother, Finn, had dumped a pile of his clothes – shorts, jeans, and one super-hero costume – in the corner of the kitchen. And several days earlier, Grandpa Quill had tracked muddy footprints from the back door to the front, with a detour past the fridge on his way through. None of the Quirks were good at picking up after themselves.

With a family of mostly magical people, the Quirk house really should have been tidier. But since none of the Quirks had normal magic powers, and Molly had none at all, not a single one of them could just snap their fingers to whip up a clean kitchen.

Nothing was that simple. And no one's magic was that useful.

Molly squeezed a giant mug into the only empty space on the table and poured herself some cereal. She scattered a pinch of sugar over the flakes. Then she dug a giant wooden mixing spoon into her mug. As usual, all the cereal spoons were dirty. And the bowls. That's just the way it was. Eventually, someone would put on some music and wash all the dishes in one afternoon. But until then, the dirty dishes were piled in the sink and on the counters and at the bottom of the broom closet (a closet that didn't contain brooms at all but did house a large collection of broken bagpipe bits).

Molly had only taken a few bites of cereal when Finn slipped one of his dirty Lego pieces up and over the edge of Molly's mug. It was a silver ramp piece, one of his favourites. Finn thought he was very sneaky, but Molly usually caught him making mischief. Usually, she was the *only* one who did.

She leaned over to whisper, "If that ramp isn't out of my bowl in four seconds, I'll tell Mum you're not wearing trousers at the breakfast table." Finn preferred to wander around the house in only underwear. Their mum had made a rule that trousers must be worn at the table, but Finn believed underpants *were* proper trousers.

CRAZY ED'S

Finn's mouth twisted into a toothless grin, and he dangled his little fingers over her cereal. "My Lego is a tiny lifeboat," he whispered back. His tongue poked a load of porridge through the hole where his lower front teeth used to be. "Captain Lego has arrived to rescue all of the flakes that are drowning in milk. Can't you hear them screaming, Molly?"

Molly fixed her brother with a serious stare. "I mean it, Finn. Three, two . . ."

Finn reached out and snatched the Lego from her cereal. His fingers left a dirty streak in Molly's fresh white milk. Molly shook her head, trying hard to ignore her brother. She watched as Finn dumped the Lego in his own bowl of porridge. Then he scooped it back out with his spoon and sucked it clean. Finn was always icky, sticky and gross.

"Happy first day of school, Miss Molly." Their grandfather Quilliam Quirk saluted Molly from where he stood at the stove frying eggs. "How do you feel about cowboys, kid?"

"I suppose I've never really thought about

17

cowboys, Grandpa." Molly made a grossed-out face as she scooped a huge spoonful of dirty cereal into her mouth. She hoped Finn didn't have fleas. Like everything with Finn, fleas were a real possibility.

Grandpa jiggled the pan. "Well, you'd better start thinking, kid. If things don't work out here in Michigan, Texas is our next stop." Penelope ran into the kitchen just in time to hear that. Her eyes opened wide and she skidded to a stop. Molly gave her sister a reassuring smile, even though she didn't feel all that great herself.

The Quirks had lived in Normal, Michigan, for less than one week. One sliver of a week, and they were already planning for what they would do when they had to leave. Molly and Penelope never went to any one school long enough to get invited to parties, they never joined any sports teams, they never even had time to make real friends.

"Why Texas, Gramps?" Molly asked. Penelope leaned against the door frame at the edge of the kitchen, looking worried.

"Why not Texas?" Grandpa Quill said, grinning as he buttered two pieces of toast. "Can you stop calling me 'old man', kid?"

"'Gramps' isn't the same thing as 'old man'."
Molly giggled. "Besides, I'm not so fond of you calling me 'kid', and you *are* our grandpa."

"And old," Finn added quietly.

Grandpa tilted the frying pan. Two overcooked
fried eggs slipped off the edge of the pan and on to
his plate. "'Gramps' just sounds old," he said. As
Molly watched, the two eggs quivered over the
toast on Grandpa's plate, then slid back up and
into the pan again. It was like her grandpa had hit
a rewind button. In a way, he had.

Quilliam Quirk's magic allowed him to have a
do-over whenever he wanted it. He could flip time
backwards, like the button on a DVD remote, and
everyone would relive the minutes or hours again.
Grandpa had long ago learned to control his Quirk
– most of the time, anyway – so his magic was usually pretty handy.

That morning, Grandpa had rewound twenty
seconds, just enough to get his eggs back in the pan
so he could take them out before they were overcooked. Grandpa preferred his eggs over-medium
– he always said that whites should be chewy but
yolks ought to ooze.

"I want to be a new man here in Michigan. Call me Quilliam. Quill, if you're feeling casual." Grandpa slid his eggs on to the plate for a second time and put on a charming smile under his drooping moustache.

Finn snorted through a mouthful of porridge. Molly jabbed him in the side with her elbow. "It feels weird to call my own grandpa by his first name," Molly said. "It would be like calling Mum Bree." She tried that out. "Breeeee. Ick, no. It's not right."

"Well, if you're going to be weird about it, call me Mr Quirk instead." Grandpa squirted ketchup on to his eggs and carried his plate to the table. Penelope trailed behind him and snatched a piece of toast off the edge of his plate.

"It's not normal to call your grandpa by his first name, and it's even sillier to call him Mister. That's a fact." Molly nodded. She was sure she was right about this. "We want to fit in here in Normal, so I'm calling you Grandpa. Or I can call you Gramps . . . your choice."

"You've got a point, kid. Gramps it is." Grandpa

Quill grinned, then pushed his plate across the table and sat down on an empty seat. He eagerly pulled the spoon out of Finn's empty porridge bowl and started to scoop up egg yolk. He muttered, "It's not normal..." Then he chuckled under his breath. "Hey, where's my other slice of toast? I was sure –" He harrumphed when he saw Penelope standing by the stove, happily stuffing the last bit of his toast into her mouth.

"Molly, have you seen your brother?" Bree Quirk breezed into the kitchen, wearing an apron with dancing chickens on it. She worked as a waitress at Crazy Ed's, a diner-style restaurant on Old County Road Six. It was a nifty place with a broken gumball machine and a rusting motorcycle with a FOR SALE sign propped up out the front.

Molly glanced at the chair right next to her, where Finn was now licking porridge remains directly out of his bowl. He looked like a dog. "He's finishing breakfast, in his own special way," she muttered.

"Finnegan Quirk," Bree scolded, using Finn's full name. She looked directly at the bowl of porridge without seeing her son. "I just hope you're wearing trousers at the breakfast table?"

Finn stuck his tongue out at Molly, ignoring their mum's question, and rubbed his face in the porridge. The slimy oats smudged across his cheeks. Molly tried really hard to pretend her brother wasn't there. She hated that she was the only person who could see him. It made his annoying habits that much harder to ignore.

CHAPTER 4

Invisible Finn

Like the rest of his family, Finnegan Quirk was born totally normal. But that quickly changed, and his Quirk appeared. Or, in the case of Finn, something disappeared. When he was six months old, he began to fade. At first, it seemed like his skin was just getting lighter. But then one day, he went to pick up one of his toys, and Grandpa Quill could actually see the toy through Finn's hand.

Over the course of his first year, Finn kept fading. He grew more and more see-through, until one day he just disappeared. Penelope had seen him crawling through the kitchen to grab a Cheerio off the floor, and in the blink of an eye he was gone. She assumed he'd somehow zipped out of the room, until she accidentally kicked him.

The strange thing was, Molly couldn't understand what everyone was fussing about. She could still see Finn. Bright as ever, solid as ever, ugly as ever. But she was the *only* one who had seen him – or the clothes that were or weren't on his back – since.

Which meant that no one else could see Finn plucking flowers from Mrs DeVille's perfect pansy bed while the family walked Molly and Penelope to the bus stop later that morning. Molly shot Finn a look, silently begging him to behave. People would notice if flowers just started popping out of the ground. Especially Mrs DeVille. (Penelope and Molly had already learned that their neighbour on the left was cranky and allergic to kids. Also, she smelled like hamster-cage shavings, but that was beside the point.) Molly was not moving to Texas because of something as silly and childish as ruined flowers.

But she knew this morning was harder for Finn than most other days. If things were different, Finn would have been starting kindergarten. Because of the way he looked (invisible, of course), he wasn't allowed to go to school. Like Penelope, Finn had been working on controlling his Quirk, but he hadn't yet got the hang of it. He was still as see-through as ever. Molly was the only person on earth who could see his sproingy blonde hair and his chocolate-coloured eyes and his dirt-crusted little legs.

"You girls should let your grandpa join you on the bus ride to school," Bree Quirk suggested. "I need to get ready for work, but he can come along and help out if anything happens." Penelope and Molly's mum worried about the first day of school almost as much as her girls did. She'd seen so many first days go badly for them.

Molly knew it would make them look even stranger if their grandpa rode the bus with them. That wasn't normal.

And yet, Penelope agreed immediately. "OK, Mum!"

"No, Mum," Molly insisted, shooting her sister

a look – the sort of look that told her twin to zip it. "Gramps is not riding the bus with us. No offence." Grandpa Quill shrugged.

"You *will* let your grandfather ride with you," Bree said, staring at each of the girls in turn. Her frizzy brown hair curled around her face, puffing up in some places and sticking against her scalp in others. That morning's combination of wild hair, a chicken apron, and staring, watery blue eyes made her mother look a little crazy, Molly thought. She hoped her mum would run a comb through her curls before her shift, since she looked so pretty when she took a few minutes for herself. Their mum was so scatterbrained that she often forgot about combs and matching socks and other things that normal mums ought to remember.

"Mum, you know your magic doesn't work

with me." Molly sighed, reaching up to tuck one of her mother's curls behind her ear. "You can stop wasting your energy on us."

Bree Quirk's magic was useful for a mother. If she put her mind to it, she could make people do what she told them to do, and could get them to believe whatever she wanted them to believe. Bree could make just about anyone see things her way. Anyone, that is, except Molly.

Just as Molly was the only person who could see her invisible younger brother, she was also the only one who couldn't be mind-charmed by her mum. Molly was immune to her whole family's magic. Immunity was Molly's Quirk, and she knew better than anyone just how lame that was.

"Are you girls sure you're ready for this?" Bree asked. She sounded sort of funny – like her voice was skipping. She was probably going to cry. That happened sometimes. Especially when she'd been doing her mind-control stuff. That day, though, Bree's tears were probably just normal-mum tears. She got all weird about first days.

"Yes, Mum," Penelope and Molly answered together.

"They'll be fine," Grandpa agreed. "The girls are in fourth grade now. And with all our moving, they should be proper pros at this whole first-day-of-school business. Quit your blubbering, Bree." Molly squeezed her eyes closed when she realised Grandpa Quill's crazy-long white moustache had bits of yellow egg yolk dripping from the tips. "And if it goes terribly, we'll rodeo right on down to Texas. No big deal."

But it was a big deal. Each one of the Quirks knew it. When they'd left Ohio after that summer's cat incident, they had all decided – as a family – that they were going to try to live life like a normal family. That's why they'd moved to a town called Normal. Because none of the Quirks wanted to move every few months. It was time to live a normal life. It was time to find a home.

Molly knew the family wanted to support her and Pen on their first day of school, but she wished they could all just butt out sometimes. There had been more than a handful of times that she was pretty sure she was the only Quirk really trying to fit in.

"I know you girls are going to be fine," Bree

said, her voice wiggling and wobbling. "This is the place," she whispered. "We're going to make Normal our home, and that's all there is to it." She smiled weakly. Molly could tell she was just barely holding herself together. Her hair stuck out at odd angles, like tangled bits of a bird's nest.

"What if we don't?" Penelope whispered, her eyes huge.

"We have to," their mother said. "It's time for us to settle down. We need to figure out how to fit in somewhere, some day. Our new, normal life starts today!" Bree said this as confidently as she could, pounding her fist into her palm to make her point, but no one looked convinced.

The thing is, the Quirks only knew how to live the life they'd always had – a life of moving around. They'd always hit the road when something went wrong. They had never fitted in anywhere, and they'd never stayed anywhere long enough to truly try.

"Go get 'em, girls!" Grandpa cried as the bus arrived. Both girls hesitated. The bus would

take them closer and closer to school. Closer and closer to the chance of failure.

As Molly looked at the driver, her stomach rumbled with nerves. Could they do it? Was her sister capable of blending in? Molly also wondered, selfishly, the same thing she wondered at every new school: Would *she* make friends this year? Would she finally find a way to fit in, to be part of her class?

There was only one way to find out: the Quirks absolutely had to make it work in Normal. How hard could it be?

Penelope Quirk often wished she were more like her twin sister, Molly. One reason was because Molly didn't have an extra-long second toe (Penelope did). Also, Molly didn't make a hissing sound when she laughed (Penelope's laugh sometimes sounded like an attacking snake). She was also jealous that Molly always spotted Finn before he drizzled syrup down her neck (Pen never saw him coming). But mostly, Penelope was envious that Molly didn't have to try so hard to be normal.

33

Growing up Quirky, Penelope had always thought she was the normal twin – and Molly was the strange one. While every Quirk had a charm, Molly was the kid with no special talents. It wasn't really until kindergarten, when Penelope's magic earned the girls a hall pass right out of school, that she finally realised *she* was the one who didn't fit in outside the house.

Penelope tried. Really, she did. But she just couldn't control her imagination.

Molly was constantly chasing after her sister, trying to distract her enough that she wouldn't spread magic everywhere she went. Sometimes, that worked. Other times, Penelope's magic wasn't very obvious. But most of the time, it was just that people weren't looking closely enough.

When the girls' bus pulled up in front of Normal Elementary School on that first day of fourth grade, Penelope gazed out of the window at the playground full of kids. She took a deep breath and stood up, following Molly as she plodded towards the front door. Molly twisted at the curl directly behind her left ear, a nervous habit she had picked up in first grade.

No one seemed to notice that Penelope was now wearing a skirt with yellow stripes. The skirt was identical to one that another girl on their bus had been wearing. When they'd left home that morning at half past seven, Penelope had been wearing shorts.

As Molly and Penelope followed the other kids across the playground, Molly was pretty sure she was the only one who saw a tiny white rabbit in a waistcoat running up a tree in front of them.

"Did you see that?" Penelope whispered, a smile tugging at the corners of her mouth. She instantly stopped grinning when she saw the look on her sister's face. "I promise, Molly, I'm trying really hard. I was thinking that I feel a lot like Alice did when she got to Wonderland, and then . . ."

"*Poof*, right?" Molly chewed on her lower lip. "Are you really that nervous, Pen?" She could sense people watching them. It was like this on their first day at every new school. Everyone always stared.

Even though Molly knew it wasn't because of the Quirk family magic, she still felt uneasy. But *of course* people stared at them – they were not only

35

new, they were also pretty noticeable. Adults *and* kids often did a double take when they saw a pair of matching girls with super-long brown hair. Big, crinkly spirals sprouted out of their heads like curly parsley. Both twins were as thin as stretched taffy and taller than anyone else in their grade. Their feet were as large as their mother's feet, which embarrassed both girls no end.

Molly and Penelope walked quickly towards the front doors of the school, trying hard to look like they fitted in.

"You must be the new girls. The Quirks, right?" Penelope jumped as a short girl with suntanned skin and a neat bob with a tidy fringe reached out and took her arm. "I'm Stella! I'm in fourth grade, too. Welcome to Normal." Stella smiled warmly at both Penelope and Molly as she repeated the message that had been on all the shiny balloons.

"I'm Molly, and this is my Penelope sister." Molly jumbled her introduction. Not because Stella made her nervous or shy, but because she'd just noticed that their grandfather was crouched, hidden, in the leafy tree above them. He looked like a giant, hulking squirrel.

Molly tried hard not to look at Grandpa Quill. She didn't want to call any attention his way. Their mother had obviously told him to come and keep an eye on them, and he always followed Bree's instructions – he didn't have a choice. Molly found it almost impossible not to stare straight at him, perched as he was on the skinny limb of an oak tree. She didn't know why he'd picked a tree, of all things, to hide in. He wasn't exactly nimble. Or slim.

"I mean, I'm Molly, and this is my sister, Penelope." She shot Grandpa Quill a quick evil look, and he grinned back at her sheepishly. Busted.

Stella laughed loudly and said, "You're twins, right? You're exactly the same."

Molly and Penelope exchanged a funny look – they really weren't at all the same, but you couldn't tell that by looking at them. "We're in Mr Intihar's class. Are you?" Molly asked, glancing up just in time to see Grandpa Quill lose his footing and slip – *crack!* – to a lower branch. Penelope gasped when she spotted their grandfather hidden in the leafy canopy above them.

Just as Stella tilted her head to look up, Molly felt Grandpa Quill rewind time. He turned time back just long enough that he could readjust his position in the tree so neither Penelope nor Stella would catch him hiding.

"You're twins, right?" Stella asked again. "You're exactly the same."

Molly sighed. This was one of the problems with her grandfather's Quirk – sometimes, the same conversation would happen over and over again. "Yes, we're twins," Molly answered. As she spoke, she quickly led Penelope and Stella away from the tree. "But we're not identical. Almost, but not quite." She and Penelope shared a secret smile. "We're in Mr Intihar's class," Molly said, again. "Are you?"

"Yeah," Stella said, waving to some kids getting off another school bus. "There's only one fourth-grade classroom. Normal isn't that big, you know. That's why we were all excited when we heard you'd moved to town. Everyone has been waiting to meet you!"

Penelope and Molly followed as Stella ushered them through the front doors and towards room six. Normal Elementary School was built in a circle, with the library and lunchroom in the centre of the building. The classrooms were lined up side by side, and you could walk all the way around the circle to get back to where you started.

Stella told them about some of the other kids in their class as she led them past the library and the school office and the bathrooms. But Molly barely heard a word – she couldn't stop thinking about Penelope's white rabbit and their grandfather in the tree and how, when she looked down, she saw that Penelope's shoes had turned into ruby slippers.

They were doomed.

When Molly, Penelope and Stella walked through the door to room six, their teacher, Mr Intihar, was nowhere to be seen. There were a few other kids milling around who smiled at the Quirks, but none were as friendly or chatty as Stella. Most people just sort of stared, then went back to what they were doing.

Twenty-four desks were lined up in the classroom, organised in six rows of four. Each desk had a different animal sticker stuck to the top right corner. On each sticker was a name. Penelope ran her hand across the desk closest to the door as they walked into the classroom. The name Raade was printed across the top of a snake sticker that had been neatly affixed to the desk.

Molly glanced back at her sister and her eyes widened. The snake sticker on Raade's desk flicked its tongue. It had come to life! The tiny snake slithered and wrapped around the corner of the desk, heading for the floor. Usually Penelope wasn't this bad. But her imagination was running wild!

Penelope curled her fingers closed and squeezed her eyes shut. She and Molly had only recently discovered that closing her eyes helped keep Pen's imagination in check. She sometimes wished she could keep her eyes closed all the time – but that was sure to attract too much extra attention. After a few seconds, the snake curled up on the corner of the desk again and settled back into its sticker form. No one had seen what had happened. Molly sighed as another one of their classmates walked through the door into room six just moments later.

"Here's your desk, Molly," Stella cried, her loud, raspy voice booming across the classroom. "Right next to mine!" Stella stood beside a desk in the front row, pressed up against the window. A lion sticker had Molly's name printed on it in neat navy-blue letters. "And there's yours, Penelope." Stella pointed to a desk in the back row, three desks behind Molly's. Pen's desk had a tiger sticker with her name written in swirly black letters.

Stella turned away to talk with another girl sitting in the front row. At the exact moment Stella shifted her attention, Penelope's tiger sticker turned into a very small, very real tiger and jumped off Pen's desk! It leaped over Pen's chair and scratched its way on to the desk right behind Molly. The tiger yawned, letting out a big, belching roar. Both Molly and Penelope coughed loudly to try to cover up the sound of a miniature beast in their classroom.

Molly's eyes grew wide and scared. Thanks to her sister's imagination, there was a real tiger in their classroom! It was tiny, but its teeth were terrifying.

Penelope scrambled forward to stand in a spot where she could block the tiger from the rest of the room. She mouthed, "I'm sorry!" to Molly, while her eyes darted to the other kids in the class. No one was looking her way, but certainly someone would be soon. This was one of those times when the Quirks had to hope people weren't paying very close attention at all.

The tiger stumbled around on top of the desk. Molly stared at her sister, then at the tiger. She was almost sure the tiger winked at her. "Do something," Molly whispered, leaning over to speak directly into her sister's ear. There was a din of activity in the room, making it impossible for Penelope to focus on any one thing. Conversations swirled around her, voices of strangers making her more and more nervous by the second. "Pen! Focus on something else."

Someone across the room dropped a book on

the floor. Everyone turned to look. For a single moment, the room went silent. In that instant, Penelope released a huge sigh, and the tiger spun in two small circles. Then it sat down on the top right corner of the desk and turned into a flattened sticker again. Penelope's tiger sticker was now stuck to the desk right behind Molly's.

Molly and Penelope exchanged a look. Everyone in the room went back to their conversations, happily unaware of what Penelope had done. Pen smiled, pleased with herself. She had accidentally switched around their teacher's desk assignments so she could sit right behind her sister. "No problem," she said proudly. "And now we can sit together!"

"Uh, Pen?" Molly said under her breath. "Where'd the mouse sticker go? The one that *was* on this desk?"

A mouse sticker with the name Norah written on it had been stuck to the desk behind Molly's. Molly got a sick feeling in her stomach. Penelope squeezed her eyes closed.

Stella turned her attention back to Molly and

Penelope at exactly that moment. She watched as Penelope tucked her legs under the desk right behind Molly, trying to get comfortable. "Oh! That's weird," Stella said. "I was sure I saw your name on the desk in the back, Penelope! But I suppose you're here, right behind Molly. This is going to be so much fun, all of us sitting together."

Penelope grinned at Stella. "I know," she said happily.

Molly tried to smile, too, but her lips got stuck and she let out a little squeal instead. Because there was a live mouse with the name Norah written on its back running straight towards Stella's leg.

45

CHAPTER 6

The Toilet S
u
b
marine

Stella sCreamed and jumped on to her desk chair and generally freaked out the way almost anyone would if there were a mouse loose in a classroom. Meanwhile, Molly hustled Pen out of room six and squirrelled her away in a stall in the empty girls' bathroom.

"You've got to get it together!" Molly cried, shaking her sister's shoulders. Penelope refused to look at her. As Molly tried to get her sister's attention, a small submarine started to emerge from inside the toilet in their stall. It popped up above the water, reaching out of the toilet bowl like a big metal sea creature.

Molly screeched, watching as the submarine grew larger and larger. Thankfully, she and Pen were in the accessible stall – the extra space made it possible to fit in there with Penelope's imagination. "Are you thinking about trying to escape our first day of school in a toilet-bowl submarine?" Molly gasped as she realised what exactly was poking out of the toilet. "What would even make you think about that? That's a disgusting idea! And you would never fit through the pipes!"

Penelope started to cry, and the submarine sank back down into the toilet bowl again, before eventually disappearing. "Maybe I should have just stayed at home with Finn," she whispered through slurpy tears. "I can't do this. I'm ruining every-thing for you." All of the toilets began to flush repeatedly – Molly guessed this was Penelope's mind's way of covering up the sound of her blub-bery tears.

"You're not ruining anything," Molly insisted loudly. She had to shout over the sound of the flushing. Molly wrapped her long arms around her sister. She hated seeing Penelope cry – it felt a little like looking in the mirror at herself crying. "It'll be fine this time, Pen. I promise."

Molly knew she couldn't *really* promise, but sometimes a little lie was her only option. As Penelope blubbered beside her, Molly tapped her toe on the tiles in their stall. She wished she could make her family fit into a place as well as the greying bathroom tiles did – in a perfect line, arranged just so. She always thought that if she could just shuffle a few clunky pieces into position, everything would work out spiffy-dandy-nice. But the jigsaw puzzle pieces of her family were just a little too oddly shaped for order.

"Yoo-hoo," a male voice called from the door of

the girls' bathroom. All the toilets completed one loud and final flush at the exact same moment before finally sitting quiet again. "Anybody home?"

Molly and Penelope both bristled. Pen was still crying, and Molly didn't know if her sister (or, more importantly, her sister's imagination) had calmed down enough for company. Molly peeked out through a sliver of a crack in the toilet stall but couldn't see anyone. She could see the empty sinks and the hand dryers and the teal tiles that lined the walls of the bathroom, but it looked like the girls were still alone – and Penelope's magic hadn't crept out of their stall quite yet.

"I'm missing two fourth graders," the voice continued patiently. "I usually don't lose a student until at least the second week of school."

"It must be Mr Intihar!" Penelope whispered. "What should we do?"

"You should come on out," their teacher's voice answered. He whistled a few bars from an old song Molly recognised – it was something their mum sang along with on her iPod. "The mouse is gone, so there's no need for you to be scared, girls."

"He thinks we're scared," Penelope whispered urgently to her sister. "Do you think I can keep hiding? Will they notice if I just don't go back?"

"Probably not," Mr Intihar whispered back. "Though I'm not as foolish as the other students may have led you to believe. Actually, I know there are *two* Quirk girls, and they *both* seem to have gone missing."

"Can he hear me?" Pen said quietly.

Molly rolled her eyes. It was obvious their teacher could hear everything Pen said. Sometimes her sister could be as scatterbrained as their

mum. Molly slid the lock to open the door of the bathroom stall. She peeked around the corner.

She could see the tip of a shoe holding open the bathroom door, but that was all. Molly walked slowly towards the door, realising it did seem pitiful that she and Pen had gone into hiding when the mouse had turned up in their classroom. If only their teacher knew the truth – that Penelope was the reason that mouse was there at all.

When Molly pulled open the bathroom door all

the way, she found herself face-to-face with the tallest man she had ever seen. He had legs the length of a giraffe's, and a torso that stretched almost to the top of the bathroom door. His head was small in comparison to his body, but the smile on his face was gargantuan.

The shock of yellow hair sprouting from his head reminded Molly of the silky hairs on an unopened ear of corn. It went this way and that, and seemed totally out of control. She wanted to call him Mr Corn, but stopped herself just in time.

"Hello there," the mile-high man said in a friendly voice. "I'm Mr Intihar." He bowed. "A pleasure to meet you, Miss Quirk."

Instantly, Molly forgot about her family's magic and her nerves about the first day of school. She beamed right back at Mr Intihar and gave him a quick nod. "I'm Molly Quirk," she said. "And I like maths." She couldn't explain why that had come out of her mouth, but for some reason it had. Mr Intihar laughed the biggest, roundest, most joyful laugh she had ever heard.

"Welcome to Normal, maths-loving Molly," he

said kindly. "So this must be Penelope." Pen had snuck out of the stall and was crouched behind Molly. Penelope was half an inch shorter than her sister, and took full advantage of that shrimpiness to hide behind her twin whenever she could.

"Hello," Pen said nervously. Her eyes were squinted into little slits and her hands were balled into fists at her sides. Molly could see that her sister was fighting to keep her mind still, but to an outsider it looked like Penelope was frightfully unfriendly.

"Well, ladies, I'm ready to get fourth grade under way. Are you OK with that?" Mr Intihar ran his long fingers through his fluffy shock of hair and lifted his eyebrows. "Shall we begin?"

CHAPTER 7

Family Style

"So we followed our teacher into room six, and Penelope went all squinty-eyed. Like this." Molly made a ridiculous squished face and grinned at Grandpa Quill across the worn wooden table-top at Crazy Ed's family restaurant. "The whole class was sitting still and quiet, staring at us, but instead of freaking out, Penelope just stormed into the room and sat down. No magic! It was incredible. After the first five minutes, all the animal stickers stayed on their proper desks, even."

Penelope beamed at her twin, clearly still proud of herself for holding tight to her imagination throughout almost the whole first day of school. Grandpa whooped and gave Pen a high five across the table.

The Quirk family was crammed into a curved booth, back in the darkest corner of Crazy Ed's. While they waited for Bree to finish her shift, Molly was sharing the highlights of their good day with her grandfather and Finn. But Finn was hardly listening – he was busy plotting a way to get dessert before his meal. They almost never got dessert at home, so restaurants gave Finn an exciting chance to practise his sneaking.

The whole Quirk family loved to eat out. Of course, they weren't made of money, so it was a rare treat. But when Bree started her job as a waitress at Crazy Ed's just on the outskirts of Normal, the Quirks fell into some luck.

Crazy Ed's was run by a woman named Martha Chalupsky. Martha had a faint moustache, cried when she laughed, and wore enormous striped trousers – but she was far from crazy. In fact,

Martha was one of the kindest people the Quirks had ever come across. She believed that her wait-staff and cooks were part of her family. Martha insisted that each member of her restaurant "family" bring their own family in to eat at the restaurant once a week. "On Auntie Martha," she would say with a wink. Thanks to Martha, the Quirks got to enjoy their first free meal at Crazy Ed's on the evening of the first day of school.

"Today was almost perfect," Molly said finally, relaxing back into the booth. After the mouse problem, there had only been one more tiny incident in the afternoon. During break-time, Molly had slipped and told Penelope that she thought Mr Intihar's hair looked like the tufty bits of fluff on a corn cob. When the students returned to their classroom from break-time, Mr Intihar's jumper had little kernels of corn stuck to it. Their teacher had stared at his jumper for a long moment before brushing the corn into the metal wastebasket beside his desk. The kernels pinged as they hit the bottom of the bin.

"Yep," Pen agreed. "Almost perfect."

Just as she was about to ask Finn what he'd done all day, Molly spotted her brother zipping away out of the corner of her eye. "Mum! Heads-up," she shouted.

Penelope and Grandpa poked their heads around the edge of the booth and watched as Bree stopped in her tracks. She had been hastily carrying a tray full of dessert to one of her tables – banana cream pie, ice-cream sundaes, a pile of freshly fried doughnuts and chocolate cake. A group of eager-looking women were watching her, their mouths watering.

Moments after Molly shouted, careful observers would have noticed one of the doughnuts slide quietly off the edge of Bree's tray. But Molly was the only one who could see Finn standing, clear as day, on one of the stools at the coffee counter. His arm was outstretched, and he had grabbed hold of the doughnut.

Finn jumped nimbly off the stool and crouched under the counter where no one could smell him or hear him or bump against him. He wiggled his little fingers and popped the doughnut straight into his mouth. Molly could see that his face was covered in chocolate and ketchup and probably little bits of his lunch, as well. There was a tiny piece of ham taped to his knee – he had drawn a smiley face on the lunch meat and turned it into a home-made sticker.

"He got me," Bree said, shrugging. She knew what had happened – she had probably even seen the doughnut slide off the plate, in fact – but played it cool. Then she turned to one of the other waitresses at Crazy Ed's and smiled her winning smile. "Hand me another doughnut, sugar, and don't ask any questions."

"I couldn't stop him in time," Molly said, putting her head in her hands. No one had noticed the floating doughnut, but Molly was upset with herself anyway. She should have been keeping a closer eye on Finn.

"You tried, doll," Bree said, swooping down to plant a quick kiss on the top of Molly's head. "I'll get you an extra-big slice of pie for that save. If you hadn't yelled something, I bet that little stinker would have tipped the whole tray over."

"Maybe," Molly agreed, flushing with pride.

"Now, my girls." Bree focused her attention on Molly and Penelope. Her blue eyes were wide and friendly and loving, and both girls beamed back at her. "I can't wait to hear all about your day. I've just about finished my shift, and then I want the full scoop, sweethearts," she said. "From beginning to end. I'll punch out and grab my tips, and then we can celebrate a successful first day at Normal Elementary School." She ran her hand through her hair, leaving a streak of sugar along one temple.

"I'm in – especially if this means we get to eat soon," Grandpa Quill said. He grunted, then squirted a bit of ketchup on his finger and licked it clean. He caught Molly watching him. "What? I'm starving."

"Me, too!" Pen agreed, rubbing her stomach. "I could eat a whole chicken myself."

It was when Grandpa slurped up a second finger full of ketchup that everything about the Quirks' good day suddenly went very, very wrong.

First, Molly noticed that Finn had made his

way to the glass case full of cakes and pies, where he was happily hiding in plain sight. Molly began to slip out of their booth, just as Grandpa swallowed down his snack. She started towards her brother, ready to pull him away from the sweets.

At exactly that moment, Grandpa Quill got the hiccups.

Hiccup!

Now, hiccups might not be a big beef for the rest of the world. They are unpleasant, but just a minor inconvenience. But when Quilliam Quirk got the hiccups, time started skipping forward and back without any mind for reason. He lost all control of his Quirk.

When Grandpa lost control, it felt to Molly like the world was on a roller coaster that couldn't figure out if it wanted to go up or down. She could feel Crazy Ed's hopping through time, skipping and jumping five seconds forward and back every time Grandpa went *hiccup*.

Hiccup!

No one else in the restaurant understood *exactly* what was happening, but everyone started to get unexplainably woozy as Grandpa did a time dance. When time was flipped five seconds back, people would suddenly feel a little lost. As soon as they felt sorted out and ready to move on, time skipped back again.

Forward.

Back!

Forward.

Back!

When time settled for a few seconds, Molly noticed that Finn was quickly taking one little bite out of each and every piece of dessert. She ran towards the glass case, trying to stop him. Unfortunately, Molly noticed Finn at the same time as Martha Chalupsky noticed something was wrong. Martha looked at her ruined desserts, and then at Molly, who was now standing by the case. It was obvious what kind old Martha was thinking.

Hiccup!

Molly wished time would rewind far enough that she could stop Finn *before* he munched the desserts. But time flipped and flopped all over the place, never stopping long enough in the perfect moment. Every time Molly tried to reach for her brother to pull him away from a chocolate pie or a raspberry crisp, Grandpa hiccuped again and set them back or forward in time. She watched Finn's hand reaching towards the desserts, over and over again. Martha eyed Molly whenever time stood still.

Hiccup!

As chaos took over, Bree ran from person to person, trying to make people forget what they were seeing. Because when time jiggled and wiggled the way that it was, people *did* begin to notice that something felt off. As she zipped around the room, her hair stood on end, the sugar caking her curls into crazy peaks and valleys.

But there was only so much Bree Quirk could do. She *wanted* to fix every situation her family got themselves into, but her magic only worked on one or two (*sometimes* three) people at any given time. Whenever she tried to stretch her Quirk any further than that, she ended up weak and dizzy, until she was all twisted up like a tornado and dropping things left and right. Her power of persuasion was downright useless in a restaurant full of people.

Hiccup!

Suddenly, Molly noticed her sister's eyes were wide and staring around. Pen's head was filling full of crazy images that were about to come to life. And Pen was hungry. Each time Grandpa hiccuped, platters of beef pies, tureens of soup, even a whole roasted chicken appeared out of nowhere. Food piled into their corner booth until it was spilling down the side of the table and landing on the floor. Mashed potatoes sat in a heap on the vinyl booth, and the chicken scooted and slid across the table on its roasted little legs as though it were alive.

Hiccup!

Things were going downhill for the Quirks – fast – and Molly couldn't stop any of it. The entire

restaurant was in hysterics. It looked like the Quirks were going to have to leave town before the night was even over. No more Stella, no more fourth grade, no more Normal.

Molly was crushed. *We just aren't normal*, she thought desperately, *and everyone's going to know it.*

Right then, the hiccups stopped.

And that was when Mr Intihar came striding into Crazy Ed's.

CHAPTER 8
Dinner Guest

"Well, heidy-ho, Quirk girls," Mr Intihar exclaimed. His loud, booming voice and shock of fluffy hair made everyone turn. The noise quieted, and calm settled over the room. Time had stopped jumping, and suddenly all the diners at Crazy Ed's were focused on Mr Intihar instead of the Quirks. Mr Intihar didn't seem to notice that a swirl of activity had consumed the restaurant just moments before he'd entered.

Molly waved meekly at her teacher and stared

around the room. Grandpa Quill was slumped in his seat, having collapsed from the exhaustion of time-flipping and terrible hiccups. Finn was dashing away from the dessert case with a chunk of pie crust poking out of his pocket. Molly noticed Martha Chalupsky studying the chocolate fingerprints that lined the wall between their booth and the desserts.

"Well!" Bree Quirk quipped, swaying to and fro. "Aren't things lively in here?" She gazed around at the other diners and at the Quirks' ruined booth, and announced, "We're all having such a nice time. Crazy Ed's is a lovely restaurant." Then Bree Quirk spun in a slow circle, like a dog settling in for a nap. She teetered and tottered, then collapsed – straight into Mr Intihar's arms.

"Goodness," Mr Intihar said, lifting her back up by the elbows. "What's the matter, sweetheart?" He wrapped his long, spaghetti-like arm around her shoulders. Everyone in the restaurant stared as Bree stood up on two feet again.

"I'm fine," Bree said, still tilting a little to the left. She nodded once, then smiled at some of the restaurant's other patrons. "Just a little dizzy."

Molly took her mother's arm and led her to their booth to sit, out of sight. Molly knew her mum was a mess, because she'd just gone from table to table trying to convince an entire restaurant full of people that they were having a fantastic time, despite the chaos surrounding them.

Fortunately, even though Bree's power of persuasion hadn't quite worked as she'd hoped it would, her fainting spell was interesting enough to get people to forget all about the last few minutes. Bree sighed, exhausted. Molly could see that her mum would need something sweet, and fast.

Like a mind-reader, Mr Intihar popped his hand in his pocket and handed the girls' mum a piece of foil-wrapped chocolate. "Here," he said soothingly. "I always find chocolate does the trick at times like this. Keep it in my pocket, for those just-in-case moments. I hope you don't mind a little lint." He watched as Bree unwrapped the chocolate and tucked it into her mouth. She sighed happily. Her hair had also finally settled, just a bit.

"Thank you," Molly said gratefully. "Mr Intihar, this is my mum, Bree." Her mother's name always felt weird in her mouth, like it didn't quite fit between her tongue and teeth.

"How nice to meet you," her teacher said. "I'm sure your girls have already told you, but we certainly had a grand day in fourth grade today. I always like to celebrate the first day of school with a trip to Crazy Ed's," he said. "It looks like we had the same idea." Mr Intihar grinned.

"Our mum works here," Molly said, watching as Mr Intihar moved to sit on a stool at the coffee counter. Her brother was sitting on the exact same stool, and Molly gasped as her teacher lowered himself on to it. Invisible Finn slid off the seat just in time, but he stayed near, crouching on the floor by Mr Intihar's feet. Molly watched helplessly as

Finn carefully and quietly untied Mr Intihar's shoes and unthreaded the laces. As usual, no one but Molly noticed.

"Martha and I are old friends," Mr Intihar said. "We've been pals since back in fourth grade – same age as you girls! Both of us grew up here in Normal and never did go far."

"Are you eating alone, Mr Intihar?" Penelope asked. Her voice sounded tiny, and Molly noticed that her sister's eyes were barely open. She looked half-asleep, but Molly knew she was just trying to keep her mind under control. "Would you like to join us for dinner?"

Molly gasped. Everyone looked at her. She couldn't say it aloud, of course, but she couldn't help thinking that this was a *terrible* idea. If Mr Intihar sat with them, how could they possibly hide their Quirks? He'd see them for who they really were.

"That's really nice of you, Penelope," Mr Intihar answered quickly. "I'd love the company."

Fortunately, their table was still heaped with food. Molly pushed the mashed potatoes to the floor and said, "We were really hungry," as though that would explain it.

As they feasted, the Quirks and Mr Intihar chatted about school, the weather, and other perfectly normal things. Finn sat under the table, occupying himself with plates of this and bowls of that, which Grandpa and Bree slipped his way whenever Mr Intihar wasn't looking.

The teacher told the Quirks about some of the town's traditions, one of which was the annual autumn festival. "Each year," he said, leaning forward excitedly, "we close down Main Street and everyone gathers for Normal Night!"

Normal Night? Molly wondered. She had a feeling the night wouldn't be very normal if the Quirks were around.

"The best part is the big surprise," he said, his eyes wide.

Molly was curious. "What kind of surprise?"

"Well, every year the town of Normal does something extraordinary and totally abnormal!" Mr Intihar explained, clapping excitedly. "On Normal Night, everyone tries to break a super-duper record.

We go after a different goal every year, and it's always something absolutely crazy. Last year, we made more pancakes than any other town in the history of time. We had a stack of pancakes that reached to the top of the tallest house in Normal!"

Grandpa Quill gasped. "Ooh-hoo! How fun!"

The girls' teacher nodded enthusiastically. His hair stuck out at odd angles from his head, giving him a look of a mad scientist. He and Bree seemed to have something in common. "Yes, it is, isn't it? Another year, we built the longest biscuit staircase in the world."

Penelope giggled. "That's a silly record to break."

"The sillier, the better," Mr Intihar cried. "It's always something strange and hilarious. And we all pitch in to make sure the record is set. We haven't failed once."

"What's the plan for this year?" Bree asked.

"That's the surprise part," Mr Intihar said. "People in town put suggestions in the box outside the public library all year. In a few weeks, the great-great-grandchildren of good ol' Herman Normal – our town's founder – will pick one. They announce it on live TV, and then we practise like crazy to get ready for the festival!" He lowered his voice to a whisper. "Frankly, everyone gets a little zany in the weeks leading up to Normal Night. And the night of the festival is really something – games, music, food, everything!"

Grandpa Quill grinned. "Sounds like a day worth repeating." Bree shot him a warning glance. When he was younger, Grandpa Quill had been known to rewind the same full-day event three, four, or even five times in a row. Supposedly, he had rewound his wedding day seven whole times. But lately, he was pooped after one big do-over, so trying to repeat a whole day now would make a serious mess.

Molly noticed that the longer they sat at the table with Mr Intihar, the more relaxed her sister got. Everything about the dinner felt so warm and easy and perfect that Molly let herself imagine what it would be like if they really did get to stay in Normal. They could have family meals with Mr Intihar, she would make friends to hang out with at Normal Night, and maybe she could even join the summer football league.

Molly was so busy imagining her perfect new life, she scarcely noticed that more than an hour had passed. The sound of her brother fake-snoring pulled her out of her trance.

"Tell me, Mr Intihar," Bree Quirk said, trying to cover up Finn's snorts. She was leaning her chin on the heels of her hands, her elbows propped up on the table. Dinner was long gone, and each type of pie had been tested. "Is there anything . . . out of the ordinary in Normal? Anything other than Normal Night? Anyone a little . . . different?"

Bree gazed at Mr Intihar, her lips pursed into a pretty pout. Molly and Penelope exchanged a look, realising that their mum had obviously charmed their teacher. His own chin was pressed against the palms of his hands, his elbows on the table. Maybe it was a side effect of her Quirk, but for some reason, people found Bree utterly charming and often copied her movements after spending time in her company. It was almost as though their minds began to work together.

Mr Intihar smiled. "Well, now, every town has its secrets," he said in a hush. "Normal is no exception."

Grandpa Quill's ears perked up at this news. He was always a sucker for scandal. "Do tell!" he yelped gleefully.

"No, no," Mr Intihar said, waving his hand. "People's secrets are their own. If someone wants to hide something, let them hide it." He paused. "But I always say there's no sense hiding who you are. Differences are what make people interesting, don't you think?"

Penelope began to giggle. If only Mr Intihar realised just *how* different the Quirks were, surely he wouldn't say that.

"I agree with you one hundred per cent, Mr Intihar," Bree said, and winked at him. "I think you're a clever man."

"I think you should call me George," Mr Intihar said back.

"I think I'm going to be sick," Finn muttered from under the table.

Mr Intihar's head twisted back and forth,

trying to locate the voice he'd just heard. "Did you . . . ?"

"That was nothing," Bree informed him. Mr Intihar – George – nodded. He was convinced.

"Not nothing," Finn whispered. If you didn't know he was there, you'd think you were going crazy. Mr Intihar looked very confused. He shook his head, sure he had heard a tiny voice coming out of nowhere. "It was me." Finn giggled quietly.

Molly dropped her pie fork on the floor and climbed under the table to retrieve it. Finn had spent most of the night sitting in the space under the booth, twisted between everyone's legs, eating everything edible that came near him. "You need to hush," Molly whispered, worried that their perfect night with their teacher would be ruined. "You know people can hear you."

"I'm bored," Finn whined quietly. "I'm hungry."

"You've eaten enough to feed a farm! I slipped you three cookies and a full piece of pudding pie." She paused and studied the space around her brother. "Did you eat those mashed potatoes off the floor? You're acting like an animal," Molly whispered. She could hear the adults talking and laughing above them. Bree's voice was raised, probably trying to mask the sound of the conversation under the table. Even so, Molly figured Mr Intihar could hear her, and most likely thought she was talking to herself.

"You're not supposed to call me names," Finn whispered, looking hurt.

"I didn't call you a name," Molly said, trying to be patient even though she was frustrated. "What name do you think I called you?"

"You called me a farm animal," Finn said quietly. He jutted out his chin and Molly saw that he'd drawn a beard out of chocolate pudding on to his face. "A pig."

"I didn't," Molly whispered urgently. "I said you act like an animal, not that you *are* an animal." She shook her head. "Whatever. Please just try to stay quiet. We'll go home soon."

"If we don't leave soon, I'm going to start colouring this guy's leg hair." Finn pointed to Mr Intihar's exposed calves under the table. His trousers were a few inches too short for his long frame and had crept up when he sat down. "He's hairy! But the hair is all so pale and shiny. It's not at all like Grandpa Quill's." Grandpa's legs were especially dark and furry, except for a few bald spots on the backs of his calves. Finn reached his arm around his grandpa's leg under the table and pulled it towards Mr Intihar's for comparison. "I have a blue marker. If I coloured the hair blue, then your teacher's leg hair would match his shoes."

Molly groaned and returned to her seat at the table. "Mum?" She cleared her throat. "I'm feeling tired . . ."

"And kind of bluuuuuue," Finn sing-songed quietly, under the table.

Molly coughed, trying to cover up the sound of her pesty little brother. "I think we ought to get home."

CHAPTER 9

Hai-Who?

The beginning of the year flew by in a rush, and the Quirk girls had started to make friends . . . sort of. The kids in school were friendly, and Molly really liked some of the girls in their class. She thought Normal was nice, plain and simple.

But Penelope was still shy and distant, finding it scary to step outside the safety of their twin-ish circle. Her magic continued to flare up, especially when the classroom was full of commotion. She often tried closing her eyes, but Nolan Paulson noticed, and teased her about it. Once, he even dared the whole class to copy Pen and close their eyes while Mr Intihar reviewed the week's spelling list – which made Penelope flush crimson. Other times, Molly would sing a song in her sister's ear to help her focus on something other than her own thoughts. But Molly wasn't always nearby, so that didn't always work.

Both Quirk girls loved Mr Intihar and his crazy lessons and zany personality. But his teaching style was a little chaotic, so the classroom was often a flurry of activity. The fourth graders zipped from science experiments to spelling bees, performed skits, and played maths games where they jumped and shouted in silly hats.

The girls began to realise there was something about noise that made it hard for Penelope to keep her mind in check. One morning, during an especially rowdy game of Maths Wars, the fish in the classroom tank all changed colour – something that often happened to the roses on the Quirks' front porch. Another afternoon, on the bus ride

home, Penelope whispered to Molly, "My body went weightless today!"

Molly, who had been listening to Izzy and Amelia joke around in the seat beside them, asked, "What?"

"Weightless," Penelope said again, with a secretive smile. "I didn't mean to, but that's how I was able to do five full pull-ups in gym. Pretty cool, huh?"

One day after lunch, a few weeks into the school year, Mr Intihar handed everyone in the classroom a piece of chalk and led them outside. "Today," he said with a flourish, "we're going to compose pavement poetry. All of you: haiku!"

"Hi-who?" Raade Gears asked, scratching his head.

"Hi to you, too," Mr Intihar replied. No one in the class laughed, but Mr Intihar's giggles made Molly wonder if he'd told some sort of joke. He shook his head. "Never mind. Haiku is a traditional form of Japanese poetry," he explained. "It has three lines. The first and last lines have five syllables each. The middle line has seven.

Five, seven, five. Simple. Today, I'd like you all to write your own haiku on the pavement for the rest of the school to enjoy."

Izzy whispered something to Amelia, then they settled in on the concrete to start writing. They waved Molly over, and she happily joined them. Meanwhile, Nolan and Raade tried – loudly – to figure out how many words rhymed with fart.

"It's not about rhyming," Mr Intihar said, patiently shushing Nolan and Raade. "These aren't rhyming poems. They should be visual and free flowing. Let your minds wander!"

Molly glanced at Penelope, who was still standing alone at the edge of the crowd, shaking her head. "I can't do it," she whispered when Molly sidled over. "My mind doesn't behave when I let it wander."

Mr Intihar came striding over on his long legs and said, "Penelope Quirk! Did I hear you say you *can't*?"

Pen shook her head more violently. "Nope." She squinted at him and fiddled with something in her pocket.

Mr Intihar nodded and squinted back. "Good."
He turned back to the rest of the class. "Perhaps
we need to work on a few examples as a group.
Let's try some 'Who Am I?' haikus."

"Who am I?" Molly wondered aloud.

"I'll tell you who I am," Nolan said boastfully.
"The best-looking football player in Normal." He
pushed his hand through his hair and looked
around, waiting for people to agree. Molly glanced
at Penelope, who had just that morning been telling Molly how much Nolan Paulson's bragginess
bugged her.

But Penelope just stood there, staring off into
space, like she hadn't heard Nolan. Sometimes
Molly wondered if Pen had figured out a way to
turn off her ears, so she wouldn't hear everything
that was going on around her.

It was almost as though she had tucked herself
away in her own little world. Her head bopped
back and forth, like a silent soundtrack was playing through her mind. Molly nudged her to get her
to focus on their teacher. Penelope scowled.

Mr Intihar swept his arm to the side and bowed,

ignoring Nolan. "For example . . ." Their teacher cleared his throat, then began:

"Shorter than the grass,

Among hills of soil I march,

I am but a speck."

No one said anything. "So?" he asked after a few seconds of silence. Molly's eyes widened. Mr Intihar's skin seemed to be getting darker . . . and were his eyes getting bigger? It looked like his long body was bulging in some places, and squeezing in others. Something strange was happening. Luckily most of their classmates were distracted. Molly glanced at her sister.

"Yoo-hoo! Who am I?" Mr Intihar asked. Molly was pretty sure his arms looked shorter and were sort of wiggling when he gestured.

Nolan shrugged. "A speck, obviously." Everyone looked at him and laughed, which is exactly what Nolan wanted.

Suddenly, Penelope squeezed her eyes closed and squeaked, "An ant?" The whole class turned to stare at her. When they did, Molly watched as Mr Intihar's body slipped back to normal.

Pen's eyes were still closed tight. Molly nudged her again, but Penelope refused to open them. Molly sighed. She felt bad for thinking it, but she worried that Penelope would never fit in . . . magic or not.

"That's right!" Mr Intihar said. "It's like a riddle, isn't it? Now, I'd like all of you to come up with your own haikus."

Molly wanted to go back over to Amelia and Izzy and Stella. She pulled at Penelope's arm to get her to join them, but Pen just sat by herself on the outside of everything. "Go," she told Molly. "Don't worry about me." When Penelope began to scrawl out her haiku on the hard concrete, Molly shrugged and walked away. When she looked back, she only barely registered that the outline of Penelope's body had grown fuzzy.

If you weren't looking for her, you might not even notice that she was there at all.

Molly was so focused on trying to make friends that she didn't realise that her sister was busily trying to disappear altogether.

CHAPTER 10

Feathery Fur and Other Mischief

While the girls worked on settling in at school, Grandpa Quill and Finn tried to find the rhythm of their new lifestyle. But after only a few weeks, Finn got twitchy and his boredom led to trouble.

His pranks were harmless at first. Finn would sneak around the house, tricking family members to make himself laugh. His favourite thing was creeping up on Penelope to drop something slippery or wet into her hair. He also loved hiding strange things in people's food – rose petals, extra salt, chopped-up crayons, toy cars – just for a laugh.

He wrapped the ham from his lunchtime sandwiches around the white picket fence in front of their house, until the whole garden stunk of ham and pickles and the fence was tinted pink.

Another day, Finn ventured out of the house and stuffed the Normal Night challenge suggestion box full of silly ideas that he'd asked Grandpa Quill to write out for him on Crazy Ed's napkins. Molly spotted him, arm deep in the box, out of the bus window on their way home from school.

With Finn, some days were better than others. But on the Quirks' fourth Saturday in Normal, things got a little . . . hairy.

"There's been a small accident." Finn stood at the bottom of the stairs, with Grandpa's electric razor in his hand, the cord dangling uselessly behind him like a tail.

Bree Quirk was at work, and Molly and Penelope had been put in charge of their brother for a bit. But "a bit" usually ended up being a bit too long when Finn was around.

"I don't think I want to know what happened," Penelope said, lifting her eyebrows and looking up from her book.

Suddenly, there was a bellowing howl from the girls' bedroom. All three kids stormed up the stairs, pushing open the squeaky door to look inside. Penelope's monster, Niblet, usually slept the day away under Pen's bed. But at half past four in the afternoon, he was wide awake and perched on the lower bunk. He had his big arms wrapped around himself, and his head was tucked up against his chest. He was wailing, making the thin walls of the house shake and shudder. Surely one of the neighbours would hear all the racket and come to check on them.

"Finn!" Penelope cried, staring at a nearly naked Niblet.

"I think he looks good," Finn said proudly.

All three Quirk kids gawked at the formerly furry monster, who was now covered in a sparse coat of feathers. Dull brown feathers were interspersed with poufy pink and gold ones. There were a few coloured cotton balls of different sizes surrounding Niblet's belly button. His body was pocked with nicks from the razor, and blobs of white glue were still oozing on his skin. "I shaved him," Finn said, stating the obvious. "But it didn't look cute – his skin has all kinds of funny bumps on it." Finn shuddered. "And Niblet looked cold without all his fur, so I tried to fix it."

"With feathers?" Penelope gasped, rubbing her monster's raw and hairless back. "You glued *feathers* to his body?"

"I found a dead birdy on the deck," Finn explained. "Remember when Gramps taught us how to pluck a chicken? That time we lived in Pennsylvania?" Molly just stared at him. Finn shrugged. "I pulled the feathers off the birdy, but there weren't enough to cover Niblet's whole body. Good news, though! I found more in the art box. When the glue dries, this guy's going to look be-*yoo*-tee-ful."

"Ewwww!" Molly and Pen cried together.

Niblet sniffled. Then he laid his big, lumpy head on Penelope's shoulder. The girls had always thought of Niblet as a pet, almost like a giant puppy, which was maybe why he'd stuck around so long.

"How did you shave him?" Pen asked. She stared around, trying to figure out where Finn was standing in the room. After a moment, she spotted the razor dangling in midair.

"With Grandpa's razor. Duh," Finn said, rolling his eyes. Molly had noticed that Finn had picked up a bit of an attitude since they'd moved to Normal. Perhaps he'd been watching too many daytime dramas on television. "Gramps told me this razor makes his cheeks feel like a baby's bum when he shaves – but that's not what Niblet's skin felt like when I shaved him. It was more like a slice of fatty ham. Yicky."

"Was he asleep when you shaved him?" Molly wondered aloud. Niblet was sensitive about stuff like how he looked. For a monster, he was awfully vain. But he could sleep through anything.

Finn eye-rolled again. "Yeah. If he'd been awake, I don't think he would have been happy about what I was doing. Don'cha think?"

Molly and Pen spent the rest of the night

comforting their monster and trying to unstick the feathers on his body. The glue was really on there. Eventually, the only thing that worked was a long, hot soak in the tub.

Without fur to keep him cosy, Niblet shivered and quivered. The next day, Penelope kept trying to sneak him out on to the deck to lie in the sun and warm up. But each time their nosy neighbour, Mrs DeVille, was out in her garden,

Molly had to push Niblet back inside. Bree brought him a space heater she found in the back room at Crazy Ed's, and they wrapped their monster up in extra blankets. He seemed to like the bonus love, but Finn was irritated that Niblet got all the attention when *he* was the one who needed to be entertained.

"I'm so bored!" Finn whined. Niblet scowled at him from his comfort taco – the Quirk term for a cosy blanket wrap – on the couch. "Can't I please just *do* something? Something out *there*?" He pointed outside, and Molly shook her head. When their mum had left for her shift at Crazy Ed's that morning, Bree told the girls that under no circumstances was Finn to roam the neighbourhood. No one trusted him at *all* after what he'd done to Niblet.

Molly caught Finn making a face. He grinned at her. "Please?" he begged. "I found a kid down the street who talks to me."

Molly and Penelope glanced at each other. "Talks to you?" Penelope asked.

"Of course." Finn shrugged. "He thinks I'm his imaginary friend."

"Not again." Molly groaned. Finn had got the family into trouble in a few different towns when he made "friends" with neighbourhood kids. The young ones would believe just about anything Finn said – they couldn't see him, so they thought they had made an imaginary friend. The problems started when his friends invited him over for dinner, and Finn piped up in front of their parents. "No more being an imaginary friend," Molly said firmly.

"I hate Normal," Finn declared, then stomped up the stairs. On each step, he shouted out an announcement. "Grandpa smells funny." *Stomp.* "Mrs Deville tried to step on me yesterday." *Stomp.* "I'm sick of being see-through." *Stomp (creak).* "I'm bored." *Stomp.* "Bored." *Stomp.* "Bored."

Molly stepped out on to the front porch to get away from Niblet's gurgling snores and Finn's moaning. She flashed a tiny wave in the direction of her fairy grandmother, who hadn't come down from the uppermost branches of the willow tree since they'd arrived in Normal.

Grandma Quirk was as small as a Kinder egg, and usually kept to herself. Gran was allergic to indoors, so she'd lived most of her adult life inside a miniature house that the Quirks relocated from town to town. When she wasn't working in the garden – Gran *loved* flowers and herbs and was a potato-growing expert – she spent her days flitting about in the backyard or alleyways. Her teeny-weeny house had hung on the fire escape outside their New York apartment, had nestled atop the doghouse in their town house in New Jersey, and it was now perfectly hidden under the drooping branches of the willow tree in Normal.

Gran was the reason they'd had to leave their last town – she'd been caught in the jaws of the mayor's especially quick cat and dragged through town for everyone to see. She'd been hiding out inside her house ever since, refusing to come down. In time, they knew she'd get comfortable again – especially since she wanted to plant her tulip bulbs before the first frost.

When Molly waved, Gran pulled her head back inside her house to hide again. Molly leaned against the front railing and sighed. The rail squeaked under her weight. After a moment, Penelope joined her. "It's too bad Finn can't go to school," Pen muttered. "I'm a little worried he's going to be even naughtier if he always has to stay at home." She slipped her arms into a hooded jumper and snuggled under a blanket on the swing at the far end of the porch. "I wish we could make him visible again. So he could be normal. Like you."

Molly shivered. Penelope scooted over so Molly could sit beside her under the blanket on the swing. Days had grown shorter, nights colder. Soon it would be winter. The Quirks had been warned that it could snow as early as Halloween in Michigan, so they'd been trying to soak up every last bit of sunshine and warmth before the dark winter took hold. "He obviously can't come to school as he is, though," Molly said with a shrug. "It's hard enough keeping a lid on *your* magic – can you imagine how hard it would be if I had to deal with an invisible brother, too?"

Penelope's lip quivered. "I'm sorry we all make things so hard for you," she said. "I'm *trying* to fit in at school –"

"You're doing a great job!" Molly exclaimed. "I didn't mean . . ." She broke off, realising she'd probably hurt her sister's feelings. "We're doing OK in Normal. Mostly."

"I'm too weird for Normal," Penelope replied softly.

Molly shook her head and tried to figure out what she could say that would make her sister feel better. Finally, she murmured, "Everyone thinks strange things in their own heads." Pen looked up, curious. Molly continued, "It's just that your thoughts are sort of, well, on display for everyone else to see. You can't exactly keep them *private*." This, Molly realised as she said it aloud, was the truth. "But your odd thoughts don't make you *weird*. They just make things a little awkward sometimes. Really."

Penelope shook her head and tucked herself further under the blanket. Her voice was muffled when she said, "You're just saying that." They sat there quietly for a while. Then Penelope whispered, "Eventually it's going to be more than awkward. Soon I'll mess up big-time. I always do."

"You do not!" Molly argued.

"Do too," Pen grumbled. "I've always ruined everything."

"Well . . ." Molly said, unsure of what exactly she could say to that. In kindergarten, Pen had imagined that all the stuffed animals in their classroom could dance – and then they did. In second grade, her mind had filled the gym with thousands of butterflies just so she wouldn't have to do the rope climb. "Just keep doing what you've been doing to hide your Quirk as much as you can, and we'll be fine. So far, so good, right?"

Penelope nodded sadly. "So far, so good . . . but I'll bet you ten bucks that we won't even make it to Normal Night."

"Ten bucks it is," Molly said, holding out her hand to shake on it.

Neither girl had ten dollars to bet, but that was beside the point.

CHAPTER 11
Another Day, Another Dinner

One Friday night, shortly after the Niblet incident, the Quirk family piled into their enormous yellow van and shuttled over to Crazy Ed's for their free weekly dinner. Grandpa Quill eased the van into the car park, slipping into a space between two tan people carriers. Molly and Penelope hopped out of the giant sliding door and headed towards the restaurant. Finn walked ahead of them, squeezing a whoopee cushion that he'd hidden under his shirt.

Just after Finn and Grandpa stepped inside the restaurant's front door, Stella Anderson and her parents strolled out. "Hi, guys!" Stella said in her always-loud, raspy voice. Pen and Molly often sat with Stella at lunch, and Molly had begun to think of her as something like a friend. Penelope still said very little around the other girls in their class, but Molly knew she liked Stella a lot. From a distance. "Mum, Dad, this is Molly and Penelope Quirk. The new girls I've been telling you about."

They all said hello, then Molly and Pen stood there awkwardly, side by side. Molly chewed her lip, hoping Finn wouldn't come back outside to find them. *What has Stella been saying about us?* she wondered.

"My parents and I were just planning my birthday party," Stella said. "You guys will come, right?"

Molly and Penelope glanced at each other. They'd never been in any town long enough to get invited anywhere. "Us?" Molly asked hopefully. "Like, Penelope and me?"

"Yeah," Stella said, laughing. "It will be fun. I promise. It's next weekend," she said. "I decided to

have a sleepover on the night they're announcing the dare for Normal Night!"

Just then, Stella's dad let out a huge belch and patted his ample belly. Molly watched as Stella's face reddened. Somehow, seeing Stella embarrassed by her father made Molly feel better about her own family. And she was thrilled about the idea of a sleepover party. "Of course we'll come," she said boldly. "I love sleepovers." This was a lie. She'd never actually been to one. In fact, none of the Quirk kids had ever been to a birthday party before, at all. "And I can't wait to see what the Normal Night dare will be!"

"Me neither. Maybe they'll pick my suggestion this year!" Stella said, bubbling over with excitement. "My mum's getting the invitations this weekend. I'll bring them round to your house, OK?"

"Um," Molly said, not wanting to be rude, but also not wanting Stella to just drop by their house. "Why don't you just give it to us at school on Monday?"

Stella wrinkled her nose. "OK . . ." she said. "See ya."

Molly and Penelope looked at each other. "A sleepover . . ." Penelope whispered nervously.

"A sleepover!" Molly squealed. She pulled open the door and hustled towards the Quirks' regular booth in the back of the restaurant, plopping down with a flourish beside Grandpa and Finn. As usual, Martha Chalupsky strolled by the table almost immediately, offering the girls a taste of this and a spoonful of that.

Thanks to Bree's power of persuasion, Martha seemed to have forgotten about Finn's dessert sampling and Grandpa's time twisting that had gone down during the Quirks' first dinner at Crazy Ed's. Though she still seemed oddly protective of the dessert case, Bree's boss welcomed the Quirk family with open arms every time they came in.

"Who likes noodle kugel?" Martha crooned as she passed by the Quirks' table. "Want a taste-o-la?"

Penelope nodded and held open her mouth. "Yum. You make good food, Martha."

"Thanks, squirt," Martha said. "It's praise like that that keeps me cookin'." She wandered off, humming something under her breath.

"Why would you ever call any kind of food a 'kugel'?" Finn asked quietly. "Who's going to eat something that looks like bogies?"

Penelope gagged and spat the remnants of her food into a napkin. She peeked at it, lying there in a pale lump on the paper, and coughed roughly. Molly suspected that Finn's suggestion had turned Pen's bite of something yummy into something else altogether.

Molly changed the subject just as their mother joined them at the table. She didn't really want to talk about bogies at dinner with her little brother, but she *did* want to gloat about the invitation they'd received. "Penelope and I have just been invited to a birthday party," she announced happily. "Stella Anderson's. It's next weekend, the night they're revealing the Normal Night dare. It's a sleepover!"

Penelope beamed, looking less nervous than

she had when Stella had been standing beside them. "We were *both* invited."

Finn rolled his eyes, but only Molly saw. "Ooh-la-la, aren't you just fancy?" he asked in a mocking voice.

"It's nice to have friends," Molly spat back. Finn frowned. Sometimes, Molly found it hard to remember that she and Penelope weren't the only ones who had trouble making friends.

"Are you girls getting to know a lot of kids from your class?" Bree asked. She pulled off her soiled apron and patted her hair into place. She felt tired and a little woozy, as she often did after a shift at Crazy Ed's. Their mother had discovered that she was a terrible waitress. She was forced to rely on her magic way too much – convincing one person that he actually *hadn't* ordered a dinner when everyone else at the table had, or another that her soup was actually *supposed* to land on her lap. Bree would have been fired after every shift if not for her Quirk! She murmured quietly, "Oh, my girls, you're getting so big. Making friends and everything."

"Mum?" Molly said timidly. "We're nine – almost

ten. It's not like it's *unusual* to make friends by the time you're ten." She paused. "It's just that no one has ever had a chance to get to know us."

"I know." Bree sighed. Then she snapped, "Dad, put the ketchup back." She gave Grandpa a harsh look.

Too late. Grandpa Quill squirted ketchup straight out of the squeeze bottle that had been resting on the table and into his open mouth. As the stream of ketchup hit Grandpa's tongue, Finn pounded on the table and shouted, "He shoots, he scores!"

"Enough now," Bree said angrily. "As if we don't have enough to deal with without you two acting like baboons." Finn snickered.

"My grandest apologies," Grandpa muttered. Then Molly felt time shiver and twist backwards, until they popped back in time to just moments before he'd lifted the ketchup bottle to his mouth in the first place.

Molly said again, "No one has ever had a chance to get to know us."

"I know," Bree said again, sighing. "I'm sorry about that."

Molly shot her grandfather a look and he

winked at her, reaching his fingers out towards the ketchup. She shook her head the tiniest bit and

he resisted squirting it again.

Suddenly, the front door of Crazy Ed's opened and a familiar head bobbed into the diner. "Girls," Bree said happily. "Isn't that your teacher?"

"Yes," Pen said, and called Mr Intihar over to their table.

"How are you, Quirks?" Mr Intihar asked. "Been well?"

Finn slipped away from the table without a word. He wound between the stools at the coffee counter, making it appear that they were spinning of their own free will.

"Very well," Bree answered with a charming smile. She waved her hand to offer Mr Intihar a seat at their table.

"Well, that's awfully nice of you. But I don't want to crash another family dinner," he said reluctantly. He was obviously just being polite and waiting for a second invitation. Since they'd arrived in Normal, Molly had noticed that people here needed to be offered everything twice before

they'd accept anything. That was the big differ-
ence between Normal and other places they'd
lived – that, and the fact that there was so much
sameness everywhere.

"You're more than welcome," Grandpa Quill

seconded, patting the bench seat. Then, just to
make himself laugh, Grandpa rewound time and
said again, "You're more than welcome." He did
this again and again, until he was howling with
laughter and Molly insisted he stop. "You're more
than welcome," he said one final time, then chuckled and let time move forward again.

Mr Intihar smiled strangely at Grandpa Quill
before settling into their booth. "Well, if you insist,
I'd love to join you for a slice of pie. I'm just waiting here for my son – his ma's dropping him off in
an hour or so, and I didn't want to be late, so I
came awfully early."

"Your son?" Molly and Pen asked at the same
time. They grinned at each other, then Molly said,
"I didn't know you had a son."

"Sure do," he said wistfully. "He's just turned
six. Crazy-fun kid with a heck of an imagination,

but I don't get to see nearly enough of it. He lives with his mum, all the way over in Detroit."

None of the Quirks wanted to press, but they were all wondering about his son. Mr Intihar waved at Martha and ordered a cup of coffee. When it didn't arrive immediately, Bree slipped on her apron, then hustled over to the coffee counter herself and poured him one. "Sugar?" she asked.

"Yes, please." Mr Intihar smiled widely. "I do miss my boy something fierce. But my wife and I split up – several years ago."

"I'm sorry," Bree said.

"It's OK," Mr Intihar replied, stirring his coffee. "Better, probably. We married too young, and two people couldn't have been more different. It's just sad that Charlie has to spend his time hopping from here to there. It's hard for him to make friends when he's only here a few weeks and an odd weekend or so a year. He usually spends holidays with me. I think he gets a little bored, just hanging around with his old pop. It would be nice if he had a friend in town."

"I'm sure he has fun," Bree reassured him.

Suddenly, she had an idea. "He and Finn could –"
She broke off, realising Mr Intihar had no idea
who Finn was. She struggled to back up and say
something to turn her comment around. Then she
looked at Grandpa, who shrugged in response.

Molly could tell Grandpa *wanted* to rewind
time, but he had used up too much of his do-over
power earlier in the night, making himself laugh.
Even *trying* to rewind time now might turn him
into a hiccuping mess.

Instead Bree smiled at Mr Intihar and asked,
"I mean, is he a Finn?"

"I'm sorry? Is who a Finn?" Mr Intihar pulled
his eyebrows together.

"Finnish, she means. Is he Finnish? From the
chilly country of Finland?" Grandpa asked, trying
to be helpful. "Finnish people are good stock.
We're Scottish, you know."

Mr Intihar shook his head, confused. But at
least they'd distracted him from wondering what
Bree had been talking about when she mentioned
Finn. "I'm English, actually. And Norwegian. I
think a bit German. There's a little of something

else mixed in there, but I'm not exactly sure what. My mum was a private lady, and she and my father passed away some time ago." Mr Intihar sipped at his coffee. "So you're Scottish, eh?"

"Yep," Grandpa said. "I'm Scottish, with a touch of Irish blood – they say that's what makes me so strange."

"Is that what they say?" Penelope asked quietly, beginning to giggle. "I'm not sure if that's all there is to it."

"So, Charlie," Bree said, rapidly changing the subject. "He stays with you often?"

"Not often enough. Usually it's just me. I'm an only child, and after my parents passed away, it's been sort of empty around here. I've thought about moving closer to Detroit so I could see Charlie more often, but I'm from here, my friends are here, my job and students are here – I just can't seem to leave Normal. Can't get away once you've fallen in love with a town. This is the sort of place people live in and never leave."

"That's understandable," Bree said, cupping her chin in her hands. Like the last time they'd had dinner together, Mr Intihar soon imitated her pose and his own chin was loosely resting in his palms.

Just as their dinner arrived, Molly realised Finn was nowhere to be seen. Her mum's greatest fear, whenever they went anywhere, was that he'd slip out the front door and head off to who knows where. Molly knew it was her job to keep an eye on him, since no one else could. "I've got to go," Molly said, hastily getting up from the table. She knew it wasn't polite to stand up without being excused, but it would be even more impolite to lose her brother. "I need to find –" Mr Intihar looked at her curiously.

Molly sighed. Finn never made things easy. She smiled and backed away from the table. "Oh, never mind. Save me some pie!"

CHAPTER 12

Molly Quirk pressed through the front door and shivered in the cool autumn evening. She glanced around, looking for her brother. Sure enough, Finn was standing just outside Crazy Ed's. He was preparing to spread the remnants of Martha's noodle kugel across the front car bonnet of someone's blue people carrier. "Finn! Get back inside. You can't spread kugel on a car."

Finn kicked at rocks in the car park. "It's a van. And anyway, I hate when I'm stuck being quiet. Guests are the worst." He hung his head miserably and wandered away on the front pavement.

"Mr Intihar has a son, you know. Charlie. He's your age," Molly yelled after him, then realised she shouldn't have said anything. It's not like Finn could hang out with this Charlie kid. They certainly couldn't tell their teacher about their family Quirks. Or could they?

Mr Intihar seemed like a good guy. An understanding man. Maybe if he knew about their differences, he could help them fit in somehow? His son would be able to hang out with Finn, Mr Intihar could play catch with Molly in the garden, and their mother would have someone to drink coffee with. "Mr Intihar's the closest thing to a family friend we've ever had," she whispered aloud. "So maybe . . ."

"We can't tell him about us," a small voice said behind her. "I know what you're thinking. But it's not a good idea." Molly spun around and saw that Penelope had crept up behind her as she stood out in the car park keeping an eye on Finn.

"But what if –" Molly began. Then she stopped. If Mr Intihar knew about them, then the other teachers would find out, and the principal would get word of it. Soon, the whole town would know about the Quirks' secrets and they would be stared at and ridiculed and run out of town – or worse.

But what if that didn't happen? She looked at Penelope hopefully. "What if Mr Intihar *could* keep our secret?"

Penelope just stared back at her, and Molly sighed. Both girls knew, deep down in their hearts, that they could never tell their teacher about their Quirks. There was a reason they'd remained so secretive over the years. Only one non-Quirky person – other than Molly – knew the truth. One person had been exposed to all their family secrets. And that person had taken off, disappeared for ever – without any reason and without so much as a goodbye.

Molly bit her lip, thinking about the way her father had been there one day and was gone the next. It was right after Finn went see-through. They had just moved into their house in Sacramento. One morning when Molly woke up, there were cinnamon rolls puffing up in the oven but their dad was gone. Molly and Penelope had wondered and wished for him to return a million times, but it was obviously never going to happen.

"At least we have each other," Pen said hopefully. "We fit together."

"You're right," Molly said with a smile. "We have each other." But she wasn't so sure about that fitting-together thing. *She* didn't fit with the rest of the Quirks. So where did that leave her?

Penelope plopped down on the bench outside Crazy Ed's and draped her arm over the giant glass bulb of the gumball machine. The antique machine had been broken since they had arrived in town. "I wish this thing worked," Pen said. "I can't get the taste of Martha's noodle kugel out of my mouth."

After a few seconds, gumballs started shooting out the spout of the broken machine. Red, yellow, blue, green and pink balls rained on to the ground, fanning out into a rainbow along the pavement. Dozens rolled into the car park, finding hiding places under car tyres and inside little heaps of gravel. Soon the gumball machine was empty.

"Cool trick," Molly said.

"I didn't do it on purpose," Pen said with a shrug. But she suddenly realised that maybe, actually, she had. She had wished the machine worked, and then . . . *poof!* Gum!

But surely this was just a coincidence. Penelope had never had control over her magic before. She shook her head, then picked up a red gumball and dusted it off. She popped it into her mouth and chewed.

Molly giggled as she gathered gumballs off the ground. Suddenly, the sound of a truck lumbering into the car park made her look up. Molly realised she didn't know where Finn had gone. "Finn!" she called. There was no answer. She worried that he was wandering around in the middle of the car park – right in harm's way. "Finnegan Quirk, where are you?" She stared around wildly, searching for her brother in the evening light. There was still no answer.

Another people carrier came rolling into the car park, and it suddenly seemed as though Crazy Ed's was the busiest place on earth. "Where is he?" Penelope asked nervously.

"I don't know!" Molly answered. "The last time I saw him he was near that car . . ." She pointed. "But then the gumballs went rolling." She looked up, startled. "I bet he followed them. You know Mum doesn't like us chewing gum. Maybe he ran off to somewhere I can't see him so he can sneak it!" She was panicked, imagining Finn out in the car park somewhere, mindlessly and happily chewing gum. Trucks and cars couldn't see him, and it would be easy for him to get hit.

"Finn!" Penelope called. She ran one way, while Molly ran the other. "Fi-*inn!*"

From across the car park, both girls heard a sickening squeal of tyres. Molly ran towards the sound. Her breath whooshed out of her body when she saw that her brother was standing less than six inches in front of a stopped car.

Molly stared in wonder. The driver had miraculously screeched to a stop, right in the middle of the car park! Molly couldn't believe her brother had been so lucky. The woman inside the car couldn't even *see* Finn. What a strange thing that she had stopped just in the nick of time!

"I'm fine," Finn called, waving to his sister. Gumballs fell from inside his armpit when he lifted it to wave. Molly could see that his pockets were full of gumballs. He'd turned up the edge of his shirt to create a giant invisible pouch for even more balls, and his mouth was stuffed with the sticky stuff.

Penelope ran up next to her sister. "Finn?" she wondered aloud.

"He's fine," Molly said, motioning for her brother to come back to the pavement with them.

"I know," Penelope said slowly, her eyes wide. "I can see him."

"Finn?" Penelope asked timidly, moving towards her brother. "Is that really you?"

Finn's face broke into a huge, lopsided smile. "You can see me?" He jumped up and down and spun in a circle and wiggled his backside. "Can you see this?" He bounced and twisted, acting like a nut.

"You look exactly like I thought you would," Pen said, grinning. She ran over to her brother and wrapped him in her arms. "You *look* just like you *feel*!"

The woman in the car rolled down her window. She looked shaken and her face was pasty white. There was a child, about Finn's age, in a booster seat in the back. "I'm so sorry," the woman said hurriedly. "It's like your brother popped up out of nowhere. I was driving through the car park, and then all of a sudden, there he was – right in front of me! I don't know how I didn't see him sooner!"

Molly nodded at the woman. "It's OK," she said. "He's fine."

"He's not hurt?" the woman asked.

Right then, Mr Intihar, Bree and Grandpa came barrelling out of Crazy Ed's. Mr Intihar waved at them. "There you are, boy! I thought I saw your car pull up." Mr Intihar tapped on the window of the car that had almost hit Finn. A little boy waved at him from the backseat. "Hello, Maggie," he said, smiling warmly at the woman. "Come and meet the Quirks, Charlie."

Charlie popped out of his seat and leaped out of the car. He ran up to Mr Intihar and gave him a hug. Molly looked at her mother and saw that she was staring – open-mouthed – at Finn. She hustled over and squeezed her son tightly. Penelope's arms were still wrapped around her brother. Finn looked both delighted and squished between them. In all the commotion, Grandpa Quill hadn't yet noticed that there was suddenly an extra kid standing in the car park.

Pen stared at Finn's hair and his fingernails and his little ears as Mr Intihar talked with Maggie and Charlie. "You're filthy," she whispered to him. "It's like you're trying to grow carrots behind your ears." She plucked at the backs of Finn's dirty ears, and a tiny carrot emerged in her fingertips. She stuffed it down the back of his shirt to hide it. "Sorry, pal."

"I'm on a bath strike," Finn whispered back. "Only Molly could see me, so why wash?"

Molly was nervous to move or speak or do anything at all, for fear that Finn would somehow disappear again. *What made him show up?* she wondered. Had Penelope's magic come to the rescue and made him appear just in time for the car to stop? Or had Finn figured out how to control his own Quirk?

"Have a good weekend, Charlie," the woman – Maggie – said, waving at Mr Intihar and their son. "I'll see you on Sunday." Then she drove off and the Quirks were left in the car park with Mr Intihar and Charlie.

"Well, hello there," Mr Intihar said, suddenly noticing Finn. The girls' teacher had his arm wrapped around his son protectively. "Where did you come from, kiddo? Who do you belong to? We should find your adult."

Bree looked panic-stricken for a moment, then smiled shakily. "What on earth do you mean?" she asked with a laugh. "It's Finn, of course. You know Finn." She stared at Mr Intihar with great focus, trying to convince him that he'd met Finn a million times before.

"Finn . . ." Mr Intihar said, pulling his eyebrows together. "Um . . ."

"My son," Bree said, shooting Finn a smile. "Finnegan. Five, going on six? Surely you haven't forgotten about the one Quirk child who isn't in your class?" She laughed again nervously, and Molly looked from their teacher to her mother and back again. Bree's smile was wiggling and wobbling, and she stared at Mr Intihar hard. One piece of her hair was sticking straight out from the side of her head, like a broken bird's wing. "You remember, don't you? Why, earlier tonight we talked about how much fun it would be to get Finn and Charlie together sometime, when Charlie's visiting you for the weekend."

Molly bit her lower lip. She knew that her mother didn't like to lie, and she felt horrible when using her powers meant stretching the truth, even a bit.

Mr Intihar nodded, his lips splitting into a giant slice-of-watermelon-shaped grin. "I don't know what I was thinking," he said, scratching his head. "Of course I know Finn."

"Of course you know Finn," Bree agreed, nodding, her hair all askew. "He's in the kindergarten class here in Normal."

"Yes." Mr Intihar nodded. "He's in the kindergarten class! Of course! Charlie, meet Finn. Finn . . . my son, Charlie." Mr Intihar still looked a little uncertain, but smiled at Finn anyway.

Charlie and Finn eyed each other. Finnegan Quirk had never had a real friend. He wasn't sure *how* to act with kids outside his family. In all his life, the most Finn had ever been was an imaginary friend. And you'd be surprised at how much an imaginary friend can boss people around!

"Hello, dude," Charlie said, after his father prodded him.

Finn half hid behind his mother but shyly whispered, "Hello."

"Well," Mr Intihar said, shuffling his feet in the tiny rocks that covered the paved surface of the car park. His foot connected with a gumball. "Thanks again for a lovely evening. I suppose we should be on our way. I'll see you girls at school next week. And, uh . . ." He paused, shaking his head as though he couldn't quite believe what he was saying. "And you, too, ah, Finn."

"That you will," Bree said, smiling weakly again. "Finn will be at school on Monday, with my girls." She swallowed, and only Molly could see just how shaken she really was.

As soon as Mr Intihar and Charlie walked away, the other Quirks turned to study Finn.

"Look at this handsome fellow," Grandpa Quill said, reaching out to ruffle Finn's hair.

"Did you do this, Penelope?" Bree Quirk asked. "Did you make him appear, you clever girl?"

Pen shrugged. "I don't think so," she admitted. "But maybe?"

Finn wiggled out from under Penelope's arm and grinned. "Don't give Pen all the credit!" he cried, dancing around happily. "Because guess what I found out, Mum? Gum really *is* good for me!" He pulled the wad of gum he'd been chewing out of his mouth. As he did, his body faded until he was invisible once again.

The others stared, seeing nothing but a blank space where Finn had been standing. But Molly watched as her brother shot a fresh gumball into his mouth. The rest of the Quirk family *ooh*-ed and *aah*-ed as Finn came back into focus again.

"See?" he cried. "It's like magic! I figured out how to control my Quirk! Now you see me . . ."

Finn popped the gum out of his mouth again and faded into thin air. "Now you don't!" He giggled and Molly watched him wiggle and dance in place. "Oh, this is going to be so much fun."

CHAPTER 14

Night-Time Truths

"Molly?" Penelope Quirk whispered her sister's name late the next night, hours after the girls had gone to bed. "Are you awake?"

She was now. "What's wrong?" Molly asked, sensing her sister's sadness from up high on her own top bunk. She heard Niblet startle under the bed, the sound of his still-nubby fur rubbing against the floorboards as he tried to burrow in for more sleep.

"I'm nervous," Pen whispered.

"About what?" Molly asked. She knew what, but she wasn't going to be the one to say it. Molly rolled in her bed, and Penelope could hear the springs squeaking above her head as her sister got comfortable.

"Do you really think Finn is going to start coming to school?"

"Yes," Molly said. "Mum's right. Now that we know how to make him visible, there's no reason for him to stay at home. As long as he's chewing gum, he'll fit in just fine."

"Yeah," Penelope agreed quietly. "I suppose that's fair."

A long moment passed before either girl spoke again. "What else is wrong, Pen?" Molly prompted, yawning. She was wide awake, but because it was the middle of the night, her eyes felt sandy and warm – almost like someone had poured the stuff inside an Etch A Sketch under her eyelids and dropped the skin back into place. She'd never tell her sister that, since she knew what could happen. Molly didn't want to risk Etch A Sketch eyes.

Molly rolled again, and Penelope could tell that her sister was right above her. "I don't know if I should go to Stella's party," Pen said quietly.

"Of course you should," Molly said. "We were invited, and it would be strange if we didn't go."

"I'm not saying that *you* shouldn't go," Penelope said. "Just that I shouldn't go."

"I don't want to go without you," Molly insisted. "Stella is friends with both of us."

"I know." Penelope sighed. "It's just . . ." She paused.

Molly waited, but Pen didn't say anything more. Finally, Molly murmured, "You're going to be fine at Stella's sleepover. Just pretend your sleeping bag is a cone of safety – like the comfort tacos that Mum makes for us on the couch. If you start to feel overwhelmed, maybe you can slip into your cone and relax." Molly's arm waved around in the air above the top bunk, drawing an invisible cone on the ceiling.

Pen crinkled up her nose and giggled. "Cone of safety?"

Both girls started laughing harder, but stopped when they heard Niblet groan and roll under Pen's bed. Their monster got very cranky if he was short on sleep. "I heard Mum say that to Gran about the garden once. You know what I mean - just that, maybe, your sleeping bag could be a sort of safe place when we're at Stella's." Molly pulled her covers up to her chin. "Things have been so much better lately at school, so whatever it is you've been doing to distract yourself and get by . . . well, just keep doing it. Don't let a sleepover at a friend's house get you all nervous. Stella's birthday party is just the sort of thing we've always wanted to be invited to."

"I have a secret," Penelope said after a moment, closing her eyes tight. "I stole Mum's iPod for school."

"What?" Molly leaned over the edge of her bunk and peered at her sister. "She's been looking for that everywhere!"

"I know." Pen groaned. "The music helps me relax. It seems like every time I listen to the stuff going on around me, my mind wanders. So I've been spending most of the day at school secretly listening to music and humming to myself to keep from screwing up. It's better than Nolan teasing me all the time for closing my eyes, but I'm weeks behind in maths because of it."

"Are you serious?" Molly felt her chest tighten the way it did when she worried about her sister. "Why didn't you tell me, Pen?" When her sister said nothing, Molly added, "You know I'm good at maths – I can help you catch up."

"I'm not *your* problem," Penelope grumbled. "I keep the earbuds hidden under my hair. Mr Intihar hasn't noticed."

"Oh, Pen," Molly whispered. "That's a terrible idea." She stretched her leg over the top bunk, gently finding a foothold on the ladder that would lead her down to her sister's bunk. When she'd settled in next to Pen, she quietly said, "You might as well just skip school if you're not going to listen. It's like you're not even there." As Molly said it, she realised she shouldn't have.

"I've been thinking the same thing," Penelope exclaimed. Her words tumbled out quickly, spilling as though they'd been dammed up for days. "The thing is, I'm never going to fit in at school anyway. I might as well just stay out of the way and let you enjoy yourself. We can hang out at the weekend and after school and stuff. They're going to figure out that I haven't learned anything yet this year when Mr Intihar does parents' evening." She heaved a sigh.

Molly buried her face in Penelope's pillow and growled. She was frustrated with her family for getting in the way and being so different all the time. She was annoyed with her sister for giving up. But mostly, she was disappointed in herself for not being able to make everything work out the way it should.

She and Pen lay in the dark, listening to the sounds of their coordinated breathing, each girl thinking her own thoughts. As she began to drift back into sleep, Molly thought about something she'd considered a hundred times before: Why had the universe or God or whoever was in charge given her no Quirks at all, while her sister was stuffed so full of magic that she couldn't contain it?

Penelope fitted in with the other Quirks, but she might never fitted in outside their house. Molly might never fit in as a Quirk . . . and *because* of her family, she was always going to have a hard time fitting in with the outside world, too.

It just wasn't fair.

CHAPTER 15

Slug-Za Party

On Monday, Bree drove all three of her kids to school for Finn's first day. It took several hours – and all of Bree's energy – but eventually she was able to convince Finn's teacher and the principal and the school secretary that Finnegan Quirk had, in fact, been sitting quietly at the empty desk in the back row since the first day of the school year. He'd been so quiet, she said, that none of the other students had even noticed him. Finn slipped into Mrs Risdall's class without any major glitches – just a lot of stares – and Bree treated herself to a king-size chocolate bar on her drive back home.

During his first days as an honest-to-goodness kindergartner, Finn learned that he was behind in reading – always struggling with the long vowel sounds, which the class had learned in the first month – and he never seemed to remember his classmates' names. He hadn't yet got used to actually *chewing* gum, so he often pulled it out of his mouth in a long, sticky strand and stuck some to his table or a wall or the circular carpet where they read stories. But these were tiny issues, compared to what could have happened.

Worrying about Finn's first few days at kindergarten kept Penelope and Molly distracted enough that they didn't have time to worry about the sleepover party. The week flew by for everyone until suddenly the weekend – and the night of the sleepover – was *there*.

Bree dropped the girls off at Stella's house just before dinner on Saturday night. She followed them inside so she could introduce herself to

Stella's mum, Heather. Meanwhile, Molly and Pen stepped into the living room and saw that several other girls from their class had arrived already – Izzy, Amelia and Norah had also been invited. The six girls buzzed around for a few minutes, zipping between the living room and Stella's room, while Stella's mum got plates and cupcake-decorating stuff ready on the dining-room table.

Molly looked around Stella's house and immediately noticed how *clean* it was. They'd grown so accustomed to the clutter surrounding them that sometimes Penelope and Molly forgot what normal houses looked like. Molly made a mental note to remind her family to clean up now and again – they weren't cave people, after all. She wished her house were more like Stella's house. Clean, tidy and normal.

Unfortunately, Penelope was thinking the same thing at the same time. Moments after they arrived, pillows popped off the couches and settled on the floor. Live dust bunnies hopped out of the corners and melted into grey, dusty piles around the living room. Molly hastily slipped the pillows back on the couch and pushed at the dust bunnies' bottoms to force them under the couch. She poked her sister in the ribs. Pen smiled, took a deep breath, and tried to calm down.

"Don't forget!" Stella announced loudly, a few minutes after the Quirks had arrived. "They're announcing the Normal Night challenge live on tonight's news. We can practise for whatever the dare is, after they announce it!" She clapped excitedly.

"So Normal Night is really fun, huh?" Penelope asked.

"Of course it's fun!" Amelia answered, flopping down on the couch. "It's the best night of the *year* in this town. Everyone comes, and it's just a huge party. You guys are going to love it."

Izzy nodded. "The dare is always really cool and super silly. I'm so excited to find out what it's going to be this year." She made a funny face. "I hope it's not pancakes again. I don't think I can even look at pancakes after last year's dare."

"Did they have anything like Normal Night in your old town?" Norah asked quietly. She chewed at a piece of her hair. "Where did you live before Normal?"

Molly ignored the second part of Norah's question. She hated telling kids they'd lived in twenty-six – or was it twenty-seven? – towns. It made people ask too many questions about why they kept moving. "No," Molly said, shaking her head. "We've been to a couple of autumn carnivals and a Renaissance festival and an apple festival and one time we got to go to a St Patrick's Day Parade . . . but nothing like Normal Night, I suppose." She shrugged.

Izzy's mouth fell open. "That's a lot of festivals and stuff."

Penelope and Molly looked at each other. At the same time, they said, "I suppose."

The doorbell rang, and Stella popped off the couch. "Pizza!" she shouted, hustling to the dining-room table. As the other girls got settled at the table, Stella's mum bustled around, dropping slices of pizza on each person's plate. Penelope got a piece with mushrooms. Pen hated mushrooms. She stared at her pizza, her eyes narrowed into tiny slits. She began to hum, a low, strange sound that made everyone stare. Molly sang along, trying to make Penelope's odd behaviour less obvious.

"What's wrong, Penelope?" Amelia asked, concerned. The other girls stared. "Don't you like pizza?"

Molly's eyes widened as Penelope nodded and stuffed a big bite into her mouth. She tried to smile and began to chew. No one else was paying close enough attention to realise that Penelope's mushrooms had turned into slugs. Molly covered her own mouth, totally grossed out. She worried she was going to be sick.

Instead, Penelope leaped up from the table and ran to the bathroom. Molly heard the door slam. "She's fine," she said lightly, trying to laugh it off so the others would stop staring. "She just doesn't really like mushrooms."

"I can get her a different piece," Norah offered

kindly, standing up. "She should have said some-thing."

Pen returned to the dining room then. There was a large orange safety cone sitting atop her head. "What are you *wearing*?" Izzy asked with a laugh. "Is that a traffic cone on your head?" Amelia, Stella and Norah all laughed, too.

Oh no! Molly thought, groaning. Penelope must have been thinking about the "cone of safety" they'd been joking about.

Penelope fled from the room. "She's hilarious!" Izzy giggled.

"Penelope is always super funny," Amelia agreed, laughing. "Where did she even *get* a traffic cone?"

147

Molly laughed, too, but she didn't think it was that funny.

As the night went on, things didn't improve. While they played games, Penelope's pieces kept moving on their own. When everyone was busy setting up their sleeping bags in the basement, Molly caught Niblet peeking around the door to wave at them. By the time they went upstairs to get late-night snacks, Pen was slumping along behind everyone else with slitted eyes and a sour look on her face. Both Quirk girls were exhausted and miserable. Stella, Izzy, Norah and Amelia had spent the night talking and giggling together, while Molly and Penelope had stayed on the outside of everything, trying to keep Pen's magic out of view. It was the *opposite* of fitting in. Molly was crushed.

"Ladies!" Stella's mum called to the girls from the living room. They were in the kitchen, hastily filling bowls with M&M's (every piece of chocolate in the bag had mysteriously turned red, Pen's favourite colour). "They're announcing the challenge for Normal Night! Come quick."

All the girls ran to the living room just in time to hear the announcer say: "And now, it's time to reveal this year's challenge for Normal Night! As everyone in the region knows, Herman Normal Night is a big deal in the fine town of Normal. Party time!" The announcer chuckled and adjusted his tie. Then he looked down and yelped. His orange tie looked suspiciously like an orange safety cone hanging off his neck. Molly swung around and saw that Penelope had joined them on the couch. She shrugged miserably and hummed to herself.

"Well, then," the announcer said, touching his tie again. "There were more than eight hundred suggestions this year – can you believe it, Georgie?" He turned to the woman sitting beside him.

Georgie shook her head and said, "I can't, Tom. There are only about two thousand people in Normal – that means almost half the town must have made a suggestion. That's what I call town spirit!" She laughed, a tinkling little laugh that sounded like tiny bells. Molly knew Finn and Grandpa Quill had put a lot of those suggestions in the box.

"So," Announcer Tom continued. "This year's challenge, which was selected by the descendants of Herman Normal, comes from a suggestion made by a young man named Finnegan Quirk."

Molly's and Penelope's eyes opened wide, and all their friends gasped. "That's your brother!" Amelia cried.

"He's famous!" Izzy seconded.

"No one *ever* gets their suggestion picked for Normal Night. At least, no one I know," Stella said. She looked a little disappointed. Molly knew Stella had put a few suggestions of her own into the box.

The announcer continued, and Norah shushed them. "This year, the town of Normal will be trying to build the world's largest ball of ABC gum on record." He stopped, then flipped the card in his hand over, looking for more information. "What *is* ABC gum? Is that some kind of brand? Or a flavour? Do you know, Georgie?"

Georgie's face split into a smile. "If I'm not mistaken, Tom, 'ABC' stands for 'already been chewed'. It sounds like the people of Normal are going to be making a big, sticky ball of chewed-up gum." She and Tom looked at each other and laughed. "All I can say is, watch where you step that night, folks! Sounds like a mess to me!"

Tom nodded, and Molly noticed his tie had turned back into an orange fabric tie. "Good luck, Normal. And now, to sports!"

Stella's mum flicked off the TV.

"ABC gum?" Stella said, her mouth agape. "That's awesome!"

"I can't wait for Normal Night," Norah agreed. "This one is going to be good. I wonder how big the ball of chewed-up gum has to be?"

The girls stayed awake late into the night, practising their gum chewing and talking about Normal Night. Penelope curled up inside her sleeping bag and focused everything she had on chewing.

Chomp, chomp, bubble.

Chomp, chomp, bubble.

Eventually, they all fell asleep. When Penelope woke up in the morning, she was happy to discover gum in her hair – and that was all. Nothing magical, nothing mysterious. Nothing at all that a little peanut butter and a pair of scissors couldn't cure.

Both Quirk girls knew their first sleepover could have been a lot worse.

CHAPTER 16

Dog Breath

No matter how well things seemed to be going, everyone knew that trouble would come. For the Quirks, it always did.

Things went downhill during Finn's second week of kindergarten. No one could blame him for everything that went wrong, but some might call it coincidence . . .

After a few days of gum chewing, Finn began to realise that his brand-new visibility had certain problems. First, he didn't *like* being seen all the time. He liked to pick his nose, and when people could see him, he got funny looks. Also, chewing gum was exhausting – and his jaw had begun to click, and hurt.

Finn also found out that school was a lot harder than he'd expected it to be. He'd never mastered the art of "sitting still", and Mrs Risdall had no trouble seeing him when he dashed across the room to feed the class fish an extra pinch of flakes during Group Time.

Finnegan Quirk didn't like to follow rules, and school – it seemed – was nothing *but* rules. He wasn't allowed to pull hair, or drop toys in people's food, or whisper strange noises and stories into his classmates' ears. Because someone could always *see* him.

So in his second week at Normal Elementary School, Finn started slipping his gum out of his mouth from time to time, just to keep things interesting. While the class walked down the hall to the library, Finn would sneak around the corner and stash his gum under a drinking fountain. Then he'd creep around school without being seen.

No one realised this was happening – until one day when Mr Intihar's class returned to room six from gym class. As Molly settled into her seat, she looked outside the window of their classroom. *Surprise!* There was Finn, standing on the other side of the glass, pressing his sticky nose to the window. The other students in room six didn't see her brother standing there. Finn wiggled and jiggled, but no one paid him any attention. He opened his mouth and showed Molly that it was empty. That's when she realised, without a doubt, she was the only person who could see him.

Finn grinned at his sister, then pointed to the whiteboard at the front of the girls' classroom. Molly focused her eyes up front. Everyone around her had begun to giggle.

Molly gasped. Mustard was oozing down the slippery surface of their board, and some had pooled in the little tray that held Mr Intihar's wipe-off pens. Apparently, Finn had rummaged through the cafeteria for squeeze bottles of mustard. Then he'd used them to draw all over the slippery board in the fourth-grade classroom.

Molly glanced back at the window, but Finn was gone again.

Meanwhile, Penelope had covered her legs with her jumper and was squirming under her desk. Molly turned around, trying to figure out why her sister was suddenly so uncomfortable. Pen tipped her head towards her legs, and pushed aside her jumper just enough so Molly could see what she was hiding. Pen's legs had turned into hot dogs under her skirt! They were that strange colour that was halfway between brown and pink, and Molly was pretty sure they smelled like roasted hot dogs, too.

"They don't fit in my shoes," Pen whispered to Molly. "I can't get them to go back to normal!"

Penelope's shoes were cast aside, and her hot-dog legs hung down under the desk like meaty stumps. Pen's feet were gone.

"OK," Molly said, her mind racing. She tried to think of a song to sing to take Pen's mind off her magic, but all she could think of under pressure was "Take Me Out to the Ball Game". Surely that wasn't going to help.

At that moment, Nolan Paulson made his way up to the whiteboard. "This looks like Joey!" Nolan cried, pointing at one of the pictures on the board. He made a funny face, and everyone laughed. Joey Pahula blushed.

Mr Intihar wasn't back in their classroom from his prep hour yet, so everyone was loudly talking about the board, wondering who had coloured on it with mustard. Several boys in the class dared Nolan to lick the mustard off the board. Nolan made funny faces, sticking his tongue out closer and closer to the board. When his mouth was just a few inches away, Nolan's tongue stretched out like a lizard's and lapped up the drawings. Penelope snorted.

The boys who'd been watching him "*whoa*-ed", and Nolan pressed his hand over his mouth. "I hate mustard!" he cried, his face twisted in disgust. "I didn't actually mean to lick it!"

"Your tongue!" Stella shouted. If anyone hadn't been looking before, they certainly were now. "Why is your tongue so long?"

"My tongue isn't that long," Nolan said, spitting out a mouthful of mustard.

"It is," Stella argued. Molly and Penelope exchanged a look. Nolan's tongue wasn't really all that long – Penelope's imagination had made it stretch out and grab the mustard off the board. Penelope couldn't keep herself from giggling.

Nolan was always talking big, but he never actually went through with anything. Penelope must have wanted to see him follow through on a dare. She hated that Nolan always picked on people but never seemed to get teased himself. "Your tongue is like a lizard tongue," Stella said. "It has to be at least six inches long. Let me see."

Nolan pressed his tongue out of his mouth. It was a normal-size tongue, tinted faintly yellow from all the mustard. "Thee?" he said, his tongue still out.

Stella pushed him away. "I see," she said, rolling her eyes. "You don't have to lick me or anything. I can see it from here."

Nolan laughed, waggling his tongue out towards Stella's face. The other guys in the class were laughing now, chanting his name. As they did, something crazy happened. Suddenly, Nolan's mouth contorted and his tongue lolled out of his mouth like a panting dog's. His tongue stretched several inches and licked Stella's cheek with a big, slobbery, flat *slurp*. He left a long wet streak behind.

"Ew!" Stella cried. "Nolan Paulson, that is disgusting. You just licked me like a dog!"

Nolan covered his mouth again, unsure of what exactly was happening. "I –" he started. "I didn't –"

Penelope's head dropped down on her desk. Molly

rubbed her sister's back. She noticed that Penelope's legs had gone back to normal. But now she'd made the class clown lick one of her only friends, just because she'd imagined it happening in her own mind.

Mr Intihar came bustling into the classroom at that moment, his hair going this way and that. He always looked a little like he'd just rolled out of bed, even though Molly was pretty sure he hadn't.

"You OK?" Molly asked Pen as Mr Intihar tried to calm an icked-out Stella.

"I'm OK," Penelope muttered, her head still down. She peeked up at Molly just in time to see Stella rushing out of the classroom to wash her face in the bathroom. Nolan was holding out his tongue for some of the other guys in the class to look at . . . It was back to normal size, but people were still impressed and shocked by what he'd done. Penelope narrowed her eyes and whispered to Molly, "He licked her because of me." She moaned quietly. "That was disgusting – Stella's my friend."

"You can't control all your thoughts." Molly shrugged. "I'm sure half the class was thinking about how funny it would be if something like that happened. Your brain must have really wanted to see Nolan do something silly." She grinned.

Penelope giggled, then flopped her head back on her desk. "Imagination stinks."

"Class!" Mr Intihar barked, startling everyone. "Now that the show is over, let's move along with our day." Pen peeked up from her desk, and Molly saw her reach inside her jumper pocket for their mum's iPod.

Molly shook her head and held out her hand, demanding that her sister hand over the headphones. She couldn't avoid listening to the lessons at school forever.

Pen shook her head back.

Molly shook harder, until finally, Mr Intihar noticed and galloped down the aisle to their desks. "Ladies?"

They both jumped. "Yes?" Molly said sweetly.

"I'll take that," Mr Intihar said, holding out his hand and holding up his eyebrows. "I think we've had enough nonsense for today. You know the rules – no music in class." He fluttered his hand in front of Penelope's face. She reluctantly dropped the iPod into his open palm. "Thank you. And I'll kindly ask that you return your shoes to your feet, Miss Quirk." He winked at Penelope, then returned to the front of the classroom.

A few people snickered, including Nolan. Penelope shot him a look, and Molly noticed that Nolan's tongue had swelled up inside his mouth again. His eyes grew wide and panic crossed his face. Penelope giggled, and within seconds, Nolan was back to normal. But once again, he reached his fingers into his mouth to touch his tongue. Penelope overheard Raade Gears ask Nolan what he'd had for breakfast that morning. "Or maybe you're allergic to mustard?" Raade suggested helpfully.

Nolan closed his lips up tight. His tongue might have gone back to normal, but he was nicknamed Dog Breath for the rest of the school year.

Tricks and Jelly Lips
CHAPTER 17 ←
Invisibility

Without an iPod to drown out the booming *clickity-clack* of her inner voice, Penelope Quirk's magic continued to flare up. To make matters worse, Pen's problems overlapped with Finn's shenanigans at school. Finn kept getting naughtier, then a little naughtier than that, until the worst day of all.

On that worst day, *everything* went wrong. And all because of Finn.

Molly went to the bathroom before lunch,

164

and found all the sinks clogged with paper towels. The basins had been filled with water, right up to the edge, and plastic goldfish were floating in each of the little ponds. The caretaker was even more frustrated when he discovered that several real goldfish had been scooped out of classroom aquariums and mingled with the plastic ones in the sinks.

At break-time, Finn popped his gum out just long enough to sneak into the gym and cover all of the balls with liquid hand soap.

After kindergarten rest time, he also managed to ring the break-time bell nine times, pushed all of the desks in the third-grade classroom into the hall while the class was in the art room, and dug up a big chunk of grass on the front lawn. The digging wouldn't have been much of an issue, but he finished up by flooding the soil-filled patch with water from the hose. The whole thing quickly became a mud hole, and several kids had the good idea to use it as a slip-and-slide after school.

That night, after Bree got home from Crazy Ed's, Molly and Penelope were forced to take action. They had to tell on their little brother. They usually tried not to, since their mother had no tolerance for snitches, but the situation was spiralling out of control.

"It wasn't me," Finn announced, after the girls had finished telling their mother about the terrible day. He crouched on the arm of the couch, preparing to launch again into a pile of pillows on the floor that Molly kept trying to pick up. Grandpa, who was dozing on the couch, startled awake with each of Finn's jumps. "I didn't do any of those things. I would *never* sneak out of class." Finn turned to Molly as he said that and grinned a big, lopsided grin.

"He's lying, Mum! If you could see the look on his face right now, you'd know." Molly stared back at Finn, hard. He pushed a chewed-up wad of melted M&M's out of the hole between his front teeth.

Bree Quirk collapsed on to the couch. "I *can't* see him, Molly." Their mother refused to make Finn show himself at home. She was always going on and on about how exhausting it must be for

Finn to keep himself visible at school all day. So he was usually invisible when they were inside the walls of their own house. Bree sighed. "Finn, I need you to tell me the truth." She focused her energy on her son, whom she could feel pressed up against her knee.

Finn squirmed and closed his eyes and tried to wriggle away, but finally he cracked. "I did it, Mum," he confessed in a rush. "I liked doing all of those things, too. And that's the truth." He hung his head sadly. "It's too boring to stay visible and act polite all day! And the thing is, when I'm *invis*ible, it's just too fun to play pranks." Finn shrugged, looking only a little ashamed.

It was almost impossible to lie in their family. The only person who could get away with anything was Molly, since she was immune to her mother's charms. But Molly was far too well behaved to take advantage of that perk.

"What are we going to do about this, Mum?" Molly asked, pursing her lips. "We need to figure something out before we get kicked out of school." She squeezed her hands into fists. Molly was trying as hard as she could to keep herself calm, but her brother made her so angry! He couldn't stop himself from being a pest, even though he finally got to go to school like he wanted. And her sister seemed like she was just giving up lately – her hot-dog legs, and Nolan's dog tongue, and trying to turn their teacher into an ant, and . . . "Argh!" Molly groaned.

Bree chuckled. "Yes, darling, I know we need to sort it out. And I will. You need to just enjoy school."

"How am I supposed to enjoy school when I feel like I'm going to have to leave at any minute?" Molly let all the frustration that had been bottled up inside hurl itself to the top of her throat and jump out as words. "I feel like no one else in this family is as worried about fitting in here as I am!" Molly shouted. "I want to stay in Normal. I wish we were like everyone else." She took a deep breath, then screamed, "Sometimes I hate being part of this family!"

That last piece slipped out from between her lips like a slimy cube of jelly. Molly slapped her hand over her mouth, trying to push the words back in. But she didn't have the sort of powers that would let her do that. The thing was, she didn't hate being a part of the Quirks – she just hated that everything was so hard. But it was too late to say what she'd meant in a different way.

She'd said what she'd said, something terrible, and now her mother, her grandfather, her sister and her brother were all staring at her with big open mouths. Penelope snuck out of the living room without a word. Molly heard the third stair squeak, which meant Pen was heading upstairs to cuddle up next to Niblet. And probably to cry.

"I didn't mean that," Molly murmured.

No one said anything. Grandpa, who was now awake, tried to rewind time to let Molly take it back, but his magic was too sleepy. Molly felt time twist and turn, but they had only gone backwards a few seconds, just long enough for Molly to hear the third step creak again as Pen walked up the stairs a second time.

169

Bree Quirk closed her eyes, then said loudly, "All of you, come here."

Penelope walked back down the stairs, and the others moved to stand in front of Bree near the couch. She stared at each of them in turn and said, "I need you to forget what Molly just said."

As Bree repeated herself three times, making sure Finn, Penelope and Grandpa were all convinced, Molly held her breath. Within their family, Bree only used her magic to try to get Finn to help clear the table or to get Grandpa Quill to turn off the TV or to convince someone to tell the truth. But she'd never had to use her magic to fix something serious – not that Molly knew about, at least.

Slowly, Penelope turned and left, heading up to the girls' room again. She probably had the sense that she was upset about something but couldn't remember exactly what it was any more.

Finn resumed leaping from the arm of the couch on to the cushions on the floor, Grandpa carried on with his dozing and Bree turned the TV up.

It was almost as though Molly's outburst had never happened.

"Thanks, Mum," Molly said, glancing at her mother. She was embarrassed. She couldn't make her mum forget what she'd said, and she knew she'd hurt her feelings.

Bree didn't look at Molly. Instead, she collapsed back on to the chair while Molly sat primly on the edge of the couch, waiting. She prepared another apology in her head, wishing she had the power to make her mum forget. But after Molly sat there for nearly ten minutes, it was obvious her mum wasn't in a talking mood. Bree hugged Molly, then closed her eyes and lay back.

Finally, Molly headed upstairs, hoping her mum would forgive her by morning.

CHAPTER 18

Rude Mood Dude

Molly Quirk woke in a mood. As she dragged her spoon through her soggy cereal, she tried her hardest to act like everything was normal. She pushed Finn away when he poked his stinky fingers in her mug of sodden shredded wheat. She tried to laugh when Grandpa threw his eggs at the wall to see if they would stick (of course, he rewound time afterwards – it was never fun to get egg grease off wallpaper). And she begged her mind to forget all about last night.

174

It should have been easy to let it go. No one in the family – except her mum – remembered what Molly had said. But *Molly* knew, and she knew her mum couldn't forget, either.

Bree made Finn promise to behave at school that day. Molly appreciated her help, since Finn's promise would give her a little break from her brother's pranks at school.

Even so, school wasn't great and Molly's mood soured as the day went on. She moped through maths, sulked through reading, and grumbled through gym. She hated pull-ups, and they had to do ten. Penelope had no trouble doing them, but Molly just hung there like a lump of clay and couldn't manage even one. By lunch, her mood was so foul that when she accidentally dropped her sandwich on the floor of the lunchroom, she stomped and kicked at it and people turned to stare. Penelope's eyes widened, watching her sister lose control.

"Um, Mol? Why are you such a grouch today?" Pen asked quietly. Molly watched as her sister's sandwich suddenly morphed into two on her tray. Her twin handed her the extra.

"I'm not a grouch," Molly mumbled. She bent over to peel her sandwich off the floor. Raspberry jam had oozed out the sides, and the bread was stuck to the gritty wooden surface. "I'm just having a bad day."

"But tomorrow is Normal Night," Penelope reminded her. "How can you be a rude mood dude when we have something so fun to look forward to?" She wiggled her eyebrows.

"Normal Night is part of the problem," Molly grumbled. "*Families* go to Normal Night."

"Of course they do," said Penelope. "Finn picked the challenge. And Gramps's been practising his gum chewing all week. They're super excited about it!"

And *that* was the reason Molly was dreading it. She was secretly worried about what her classmates would think when they saw her family. What if Grandpa time-twisted and spun everyone through space, until no one knew when or where they were any more? What if Penelope panicked and made the ABC gumball explode? What if their mother used her magic so much that she spun until her hair wrapped into a tangled mess on top of her head? What if Finn did one of the *zillion* things he could do to make mischief? And what if Molly couldn't cover it all up?

Molly felt guilty about saying she wished she wasn't a Quirk, but she felt even guiltier that – deep down – she wished she could hide her family from everyone forever. She didn't say any of that, but Penelope understood. "Oh," Pen said, tipping her head down low. "You think we're going to screw up really badly, don't you?"

"How are we, ladies?" Mr Intihar suddenly appeared, towering above Molly and Penelope as Molly worked to scrape the remnants of her sandwich off the floor. Bits of napkin were stuck to the jam, and now there was just a big pile of mess on the floor. "Are we looking forward to Normal Night tomorrow?" He lifted his eyebrows expectantly. "I hope that charming mother of yours will be joining us?"

"Yeah," Pen said nervously. "Mum's coming."

"And the rest of your family? Charlie's going to be here, and I'm hoping he and Finn can spend

some time together," Mr Intihar said. He was balancing his lunch tray awkwardly, and Molly watched as his milk carton began to slide towards the centre of his tray. If it kept sliding, it was going to tip everything off balance and their teacher's lunch would join Molly's sandwich on the floor.

But then, as if by magic, the milk carton grew tiny little legs and waddled back to the outer edge of his tray again. Penelope shot Molly an apologetic look. Mr Intihar continued, "This will be a good chance for your family to get to know some of the other folks in Normal."

Molly grimaced. "That'll be great," she said, but didn't mean it. She didn't want her family to meet anyone. She wanted them to stay tucked back behind the fence with its hammy paint and just keep to themselves. If her family suddenly started prancing around town, making themselves noticeable, that would be the end of Normal. She was sure of it. And she knew Penelope knew it, too.

CHAPTER 19

NoT-SO-nOrMaL nIgHt

Even through the haze of her continuing bad mood, Molly Quirk marvelled at how magical and perfect their town looked on Normal Night. The entire village had been turned into a kind of fairyland at twilight.

As the Quirk family walked through the neighbourhood towards the town centre, strings of lights dripped from the trees along the pavements, sprinkling twinkling colours all around them. Even Gran was curious, so the kids' fairy grandmother flitted behind the rest of the family, tucking up into trees where her wings glowed and glinted in the reflection from the lights.

The centre streets had all been closed to car and truck traffic, and the roadways were open for walking. So the Quirks meandered from their house towards the town square, trotting up the centre of the street. Everything was quiet and still around them, though they could hear the buzz and hum of the huge party ahead. They admired the identical houses that were lined up like soldiers on either side of them. And they marvelled at the trees that all bowed and swayed from exactly the same height over their heads.

A WELCOME TO NORMAL banner hung between two street lamps and stretched through the air above them as they approached the centre square. "It's like a door," Finn observed, chomping and smacking at the gum in his mouth. "A doorway to Normal."

Grandpa snickered. "Or a magic portal! You walk under that banner and – *zap!* – you become normal. Wouldn't that be something?"

"I wish it worked that way," Molly muttered. Her mother gave her a warning look.

Grandpa Quill lifted his feet and danced merrily along, his moustache leaping and swaying with each hop. "Eh," he said happily. "Normal's overrated. Being just like everyone else is boring."

Molly wasn't sure she agreed.

Finn pulled his gum out of his mouth like it was a long, wiggly tightrope and then pushed it back in again. "Now you see me," he chanted, before he spat the rope of gum into his filthy palm. "Now you don't!" Finn giggled and skipped along, moving the gum between his mouth and his palm, seemingly unconcerned that they were in public and that he was weaving in and out of focus.

"Finnegan Quirk, is that a pair of underwear on your head?" their mother demanded as Finn swerved into view for the fourth time. Molly had stopped watching him, preferring instead to admire the sameness that surrounded them on their walk through the town's streets. Penelope was humming softly beside her twin, lost in her

own thoughts. "Tell me the truth! It's underwear, isn't it?"

Molly groaned. Underwear on Finn's head was the least of their worries. "Can't you all, please, just try to keep your Quirks quiet tonight?" she begged them. "No disappearing; no rewinding – or, for that matter, dancing; and no tricking people into thinking things they should not be thinking. No Quirkiness, at all." Out of the corner of her eye, Molly spotted Gran zipping away, back towards their house. The others all nodded sombrely, but their promises didn't make Molly feel any less anxious.

No one said anything more as they walked the rest of the way towards the festival. Molly could feel the tension in the air. Penelope's nerves swirled around them like bees – buzzing just close enough that it was disturbing.

The centre square was even more festive than the streets that surrounded it. Lights hung from every available surface, and carnival games were squeezed into the tiniest spaces between the shops. The smell of food wafted from grills and portable ovens and deep fryers, and the sweet sugariness of candyfloss mingled with the saltiness of roasted nuts in the most perfect way. There were people everywhere, eating, talking, laughing – and they were all chewing gum.

As the Quirks zigzagged through the crowds towards the town's true centre, Molly spotted a giant golden platter sitting on top of a pedestal, right in the middle of everything. Finn dashed off to explore the carnival, and Bree and Grandpa headed towards one of the food booths. Molly pulled Penelope towards the golden platter and they both peered at it curiously. There was a sticky-looking multicoloured lump in the centre. "Is that the ball of gum?" Molly wondered aloud.

"Yeah! That's the start of the ABC ball!" Stella's voice rang out behind them, and both girls turned to see some of their friends from school standing right beside them, chewing rapidly. "It's already a decent size, isn't it?" Stella asked. She spat the gum out of her mouth and pressed it on to the top of the pile in the centre of the platter. Then she popped another gumball out of her pocket and got back to work. "But it needs to be, like, a hundred times bigger than that to beat the record."

"Hey," Amelia blurted out, looking closely at Molly and Penelope. "You better get some gum and start chewing. When it's nice and sticky, add your piece to the pile and start on another one."

Molly and Penelope followed their friends to a huge gumball machine sitting in the centre of the square. It was the very same one that had been sitting, broken, outside Crazy Ed's until the night Penelope made it explode. Now it seemed to work just fine. Boxes of gumballs and packages of gum were stacked up beside the gumball machine, waiting for their turn to be chewed.

Each of the Quirk girls turned the crank to release a gumball. They began to chew and joined their friends as they wandered around the square – stopping periodically to place their chewed-up gum in the pile at the centre of the golden platter.

After only a few minutes of wandering, Penelope's mind began to race. She discovered she couldn't even be near the dunk tank, because the ball seemed to always hit its target and send people screaming into the icy water below. She also found it was hard to blend in when she *played* carnival games, since her balls or darts or beanbags always landed exactly where they were supposed to land to win prizes. After just an hour of playing, Penelope had won a stuffed shark, a dancing monkey and a broken plastic gumball machine (which she gave to Finn).

About half past seven, a band began to play on the big stage that had been set up outside the post office.

They played strange songs, the sort of twangy, goopy love junk that Bree Quirk always listened to. Molly and Penelope watched as their mother joined Mr Intihar in the big open area that had been roped off for dancing. Bree looked like she was having a great time, despite her embarrassing flopping and hopping that was supposed to be dancing. She seemed to have charmed the people around her, even though she looked a little bit like a hooked fish.

"Attention!" someone squawked into a microphone just a few minutes after eight. "May I have your attention, please?"

Everyone turned to the stage. The mayor of Normal, Michelle Normal, was chomping her gum so loudly that each *snap* and *pop* echoed through the loud speakers. "Good evening, everyone!" Mayor Normal cried, and everyone cheered. "It's the big night, the night we wait for all year! Normal Night is here again!" She clapped and chewed, then spat her gum into her palm and started in on a new piece.

"As you all know, this night is a celebration of

who we are! Let's hear it for Normal and our not-so-normal record-breaking!" Everyone clapped and whooped, and Molly couldn't keep herself from smiling as she blended into the crowd of cheering people. She looked around at the people who surrounded her – new friends, and her family, and all the people in the community. Finn and Mr Intihar's son, Charlie, were messing about near the dunk tank. Bree was laughing quietly with the girls' teacher nearby on the dance floor. And Grandpa had made his way up onstage, where he'd joined the band as an unofficial accordion player.

Stella caught Molly's eye and smiled at her. Molly smiled back, and Molly felt – for a fleeting moment – exactly what it would be like to fit in somewhere. To be a part of something.

Mayor Normal cleared her throat and continued. "Now, we're not even halfway to our goal . . . so we've got a lot of chewing to do. Make sure you get your gum nice and sticky, and plop it on the pile. Every piece needs to stick, or this isn't going to happen, people!" She paused and

spat her second piece of gum into her palm –
then started on yet another. "Like every year, we
have until ten o'clock to reach our goal. I have
faith that we can build the largest ball of ABC
gum ever!"

Everyone cheered again and Mayor Normal
gave the band a signal to resume playing. Molly
watched as the mayor stepped off the stage and
made her way to the giant golden platter to drop
the gum she'd put in her hand on to the growing
pile. She pulled and tugged, but the gum seemed
to be stuck to her skin. Molly turned to her sister
and saw that Penelope had narrowed her eyes and
was trying hard to distract herself.

"It's stuck, isn't it?" Molly asked her quietly. She
noticed that her own gum had grown extra-sticky
in her mouth. "Is the gum stuck to the mayor's
hand?"

"I'm sorry," Penelope whispered. "I was just a
little worried that the gum wouldn't be sticky
enough to make the ball work! I couldn't stop
myself from thinking about it." Pen could hardly
open her mouth, since the piece of gum she'd been

chewing was sticking to her teeth, her tongue and the roof of her mouth. Molly looked around and saw that every mouth around her was working extra hard to chew. Everyone's gum had grown stickier and stickier as the mayor spoke. Penelope looked terrified. "Distract me, or I'm going to ruin the challenge for everyone!"

Molly rubbed her sister's hand. "Come on," she urged. "Let's go and add our gum to the ball and get your mind on something else."

She led her sister towards the golden platter. Both girls reached toward the pile to drop their chewed-up gum on to the disgusting, sticky mess. Several other people came over at the same time, and they all pressed their pieces of gum into place . . . and then got stuck.

"My hand is stuck!" cried a woman with bright-red hair and giant spectacles. Molly recognised her as someone who worked at the post office. The woman looked around desperately, pulling and tugging at her hand, but it obviously wasn't going anywhere. The golden bangles that Post Office Lady was wearing around her arm slipped down

191

her wrist and stuck to the gum, too. "My hand! My bracelets!"

Molly and Penelope were both stuck, as was Raade Gears, from their class, and his younger sister. A few people who were nearby came over to try to help, but they were pulled towards the ball of gum as if by a magnetic, gummy force. Soon, dozens of people were stuck.

"This is a disaster!" Molly hissed. "Pen, you've got to calm down. Think of something else. Anything else!"

Grandpa sidled up behind the girls. "Do you mind if I help?" he asked Molly.

"Please, Gramps," Molly whispered, realising her grandfather was the only person who could fix the pickle they were in. "We need you."

"So you're saying you *do* want me to use my Quirk?" Grandpa asked with a smirk. "Huh . . . I thought magic was off-limits tonight?"

Molly *had* said that, but now she realised that a little magic might be necessary. "Go ahead," she said with a weak smile.

Grandpa Quill grinned, twisted the ends of his moustache and patted Molly on the back.

Post Office Lady looked at the Quirks, her eyes bulging out beneath her giant glasses. She pulled her eyebrows together, opened her mouth wide and cried, "Did I hear you say magic?! What magic?"

CHAPTER 20

Molly Quirk's Quirk

Just as eVeryone in Normal turned to stare, Molly felt time shifting and twisting and wiggling backwards. Nanoseconds later, they were back where they had been a few minutes before, listening to Mayor Normal give her speech – again. Just before she spat her second piece of gum into her fist, Molly grabbed her sister's hand and began to sing a song. She also pressed her hand over her sister's eyes to crowd out her vision. Molly sang loudly enough that Penelope was completely

194

distracted, and also loudly enough that everyone around them turned to shush her.

This time, the mayor finished her speech – "... I have faith that we can build the largest ball of ABC gum ever!" – without any trouble. Then she walked over to the golden platter and dropped her gum on the pile without further incident.

Molly waved gratefully at her grandfather. He was back up onstage with the band, happily playing the accordion. She hoped they wouldn't need to use his Quirk again.

The next half-hour or so went along smoothly. Molly and Penelope trailed after their friends as they played games. Finn and Bree disappeared into the crowd with Mr Intihar and Charlie. And Grandpa went wild onstage with the band.

After a while, Mayor Normal stepped back up onstage to make another announcement. "Good folks of Normal! I hope everyone's having a great time," she called out, waving. "I'm afraid we've run into a slight problem." She cleared her throat as a curious murmur rose from the crowd. Molly and Penelope exchanged nervous glances.

"This is a bit of a . . . ah . . . shall we say *sticky* situation?" Mayor Normal laughed, but it was more of an uncomfortable chuckle than a pleased sort of sound. "It's rather embarrassing, actually. The thing is, we seem to be running out of gum."

Everyone spoke in hushed tones at once – almost as if they'd practised it. "What are they going to do?" Penelope asked.

"I don't know." Molly shrugged. "Get more?"

"The trouble is," Mayor Normal continued, her microphone squeaking, "we've bought up the entire county. Every last piece of gum within forty miles was dedicated to tonight's goal. And we seem to have chewed our way through it." She shuffled her feet nervously. "We have a few pieces left in the gumball machine – but unless there's some sort of miracle, it looks like we may not achieve our goal this year, folks. The record might go unbroken."

The people of Normal sighed in unison.

Suddenly, Molly had an idea. She tugged Penelope into a darkened, empty space behind the fresh veggie stand and looked her sister right in

196

the eyes. "You can fix this," she told Penelope. "You're going to be the hero of Normal Night."

"No, I'm not," Penelope replied glumly. "We're trying to fit in, not stick out. We need to act *less* like ourselves, right?"

Molly smiled, hearing her own words repeated back. Sometimes she and Penelope were so in sync, but still so different. It was as though they were meant to be one girl, but that one girl had split in their mother's womb and come out as two instead. Penelope had got the family's Quirkiness. And Molly got . . . *what*?

Then it hit her. Molly suddenly knew what that *what* was. Though there wasn't anything spectacular or exciting or flashy about her, she suddenly realised she did have a place in her family. An important place. It was just that her "Quirk" – if you could even call it that – was a different kind of magic.

"Pen?" Molly said quietly, watching as her sister chewed her lip and tried to keep herself from crying. Molly took a deep breath and soldiered on. "Your mind has the power to make

197

things happen. You know that. Now, tonight, you need to stop worrying about what might go wrong because of your imagination and focus on the good things you can do. Can you do that?"

Penelope looked at her sister like she was a little crazy. "I've never controlled my thoughts before. I'm only just starting to get the hang of *stopping* my magic," she said sadly. "And I can't even do that right."

"I think you do more right than you realise," Molly said, blooming with confidence. "Remember the gumball machine at Crazy Ed's? I have a feeling that wasn't just an accident. Maybe you made the gumballs run all over the place for a reason. If you hadn't, we might never have figured out how to make Finn visible, right? I have a feeling that if you decide that our town needs more gum, we can have more gum. Just close your eyes and picture what you want. You need to believe in yourself!"

Both girls stood in the quiet space between buildings, with Molly fixated on Penelope as Pen closed her eyes and took a deep breath. Suddenly, a spotted pony strolled up behind them and nudged Molly in the rear end.

"Focus, Pen!"

Penelope looked at the pony wistfully, then closed her eyes again.

"You can do this, Penelope. This is our chance to save Normal Night. You can make more gum appear - enough that our town can still win this thing. I just know it. The Quirks can save Normal Night!" Molly focused her energy on making her sister believe in herself. Even though Pen couldn't always control her magic - and still hadn't quite figured out how to stop things from happening when her mind really, really wanted them to - maybe there was a reason. Maybe it was Molly's job to make Penelope believe her magic was something special. To make her believe in herself.

Molly Quirk had been working so hard to hide her family's Quirks that she had never let herself consider just how useful their magic could be. In the five years since their dad had disappeared, they had been focusing all their effort on trying to be just like everyone else – and failing miserably. Maybe it was time to look at things a little differently. Perhaps they didn't need to hide their magic . . . they just had to use it in a better way!

It was possible, even, that everyone would be better off if they played up their differences! She was going to help her family put their Quirks to good use, no matter what. Because of her immunity, it was the one thing Molly knew she could do that no one else could.

"Focus, Pen," she said again. "You've got to believe it's what you really want."

Penelope squeezed her eyes tight and let her mind meander through fields of gum – small balls, large balls, sticks and squares. Pink, yellow, green, white, blue and violet. She

imagined gum filling the gumball machine, stuffing the boxes around it, and flowing out of the drainpipes. She imagined enough gum to keep the whole town chewing for years.

Both girls startled at the sound of loud pops nearby, like hail hitting a tin roof – sudden, sharp, and continuous. "Do you think it worked?" Penelope asked.

Molly shrugged as the noise subsided. "Dunno. Let's go and check it out."

They walked back out to the centre square. It was total chaos. Everyone was looking around for the source of the popping sounds. Finn ran up to his sisters, his mouth stuffed with gum. "You guys? I think you should come and check out the dunk tank . . ."

Penelope and Molly ran after Finn. Mrs Owens, the school media teacher, had closed down the dunk tank line nearly an hour earlier. She'd told everyone the tank was broken, but Molly and Penelope knew that it wasn't. It was just that Pen's imagination had made the person sitting above the tank fall into the cold water on every single turn.

"Look!" Finn cried, standing on tiptoes to peek over the edge of the tank. Instead of an icy pool of water, the whole thing was filled with hundreds of gumballs!

The Quirk kids stared down into the tank. "I did it!" Penelope exclaimed.

"You did it," Molly agreed, grinning. "The question is, how are we going to explain how all of this gum got here? It's not like we can fool anyone that more gum was hiding out in the dunk tank the whole time."

Suddenly, a tiny voice piped up from deep inside the pit of gum. "Help!" the voice cried. "I'm stuck!"

CHAPTER 21

The Final Piece

"Is that the gum talking?" Penelope wondered aloud.

Finn rolled his eyes. "That's just Charlie – Mr Intihar's son." He shrugged. "We were playing a game."

"A game in the dunk tank?" Molly asked.

Finn grinned. "Yeah. Charlie sits on the seat. Then I push the button to make him fall. Splash!" He laughed hilariously. "We did it, like, a hundred times."

"He let you dunk him a hundred times?" Penelope gasped.

"He didn't *know* it was me," Finn answered. "I popped my gum out when I pushed the button. I didn't want him to see me. Charlie probably thinks the dunk tank is magic or something!"

Molly and Penelope shared a glance. "OK . . ." Molly said finally. "We need to get Charlie out of there, and we need to figure out some way to get this gum out of the dunk tank and into the gumball machine without anyone seeing us."

"Can't we just have Mum tell everyone that the gum was hiding in here all along?" Finn suggested. "People always believe her, you know. She's very clever."

Just then, Bree Quirk appeared and began to shake her head. "I can't do that," she said certainly. "I can't convince this many people to believe something – you know my magic doesn't stretch that far. I wish I *could*."

"It doesn't matter, Mum," Molly said as a thought formed in her head. "I've got a different idea. What we really need is for you to convince

Charlie to forget about the gum in the dunk tank. Then, get him to stay away from here for a while. You can do that, right?"

Bree nodded. "That much I can certainly do." All of the Quirks helped dig Charlie out of the gum. Moments later, Charlie listened as Bree Quirk told him an elaborate story about what he'd *really* been doing for the past hour or so – getting ready for the championship round in the bouncy castle highest-jump competition. Charlie, looking excited, scuttled off to rejoin the festival while the Quirk kids went to work. Bree made her way towards the bouncy castle to convince the teenagers who were in charge to actually *have* a jumping contest.

"OK," Molly said, pulling her brother and sister into a huddle. "Here's the plan. Finn, you're going to pull the gum out of your mouth, then sneak the gumballs from the dunk tank to the gumball machine. If you fill it up slowly, no one will notice that we're doing it. It will just look like the gumball machine's not getting any emptier, even though people keep taking the gum."

A slow smile spread over Finn's face. "So you're

telling me I'm *supposed* to get invisible in public and sneak around?" He began to laugh. "I love this plan!"

Finn snuck behind the dunk tank, and when he re-emerged, his gum was out of his mouth and behind his ear. "I put the chewed-up piece back here," he explained to Molly, who could still see him. "I didn't want it to go to waste – every piece counts, right? I'll add it to the ball when I run up there."

"Just be careful," Molly said, but she knew she didn't have to worry. Her brother had had plenty of practice being sneaky, and since it was his challenge they were working towards that night, she knew he wanted to succeed more than anyone else. He hid the gumballs inside his invisible shirt, so no one would see them floating through the air as he passed.

Molly and Penelope ran towards the gumball machine. Their job was to distract people every time Finn came trotting towards them with another delivery of gumballs. Molly would quietly lift the lid on the top of the machine just in time for her brother to dump in another load, and then she dropped it back into place again. In just fifteen minutes, Finn had carried more than twenty loads of gumballs from the dunk tank to the gumball machine. Even though the ABC ball continued to get bigger, and people kept chewing, the supply of gum didn't seem to be getting any smaller.

"Molly," Penelope whispered happily, through a mouthful of gum. "Your plan is going to work! No one is noticing."

Molly chewed and popped, chewed and spat, growing more excited by the moment. She watched as Mayor Normal measured the ball, then remeasured, and measured again. With each piece of gum that was stuck on to the ball, Mayor Normal's smile got wider, until she began to look positively giddy.

Through everyone's chewing and early celebrations, Finn continued to sneak gumballs from the dunk tank to the gumball machine. Molly watched him dodge and weave through the crowd, carrying loads of colourful gumballs in his shirt pouch until finally, the dunk tank was empty.

But the gumball machine was nearly empty,

too. Finn pulled the sticky piece of gum from behind his ear and smushed it on to the pile. Then he just managed to snag one of the last remaining fresh gumballs for himself before they were all gone. He dodged back behind the dunk tank, popped the gum into his mouth, and made himself visible again so he could rejoin the party.

Molly and Penelope both gave him a high five as he wiggled with pride. "You did it!" Molly said, beaming. "No one suspects anything – and it's almost ten o'clock. We must be so close to breaking the record!"

Just as she said that, Mayor Normal stepped back up onstage again. "Well, folks," she said, shaking her head. "I don't know how it's possible, but our gum supply has survived the night." Everyone cheered, but no one yelled as loudly as Penelope and Molly and Finnegan Quirk. "I need everyone to put their very last piece on the pile, and then let's measure this sticky beauty to see if we broke this year's not-so-normal record!"

The townspeople all gathered around the golden platter and reached their hands towards the pile of gum. Wad after wad was pressed on to the huge, sticky lump, until finally every last piece for forty miles around – and some from Pen's own imagination – was added to the ball. Mayor Normal stepped off the stage, and everyone grew quiet as they waited for her to announce the result.

The mayor approached the ball of gum and stretched her tape measure from here to there, around and down, then up and back. No one said a word. In fact, Penelope could hardly even breathe while they waited for the mayor to tell them the good news. Molly was buzzing with excitement – they'd been a part of something important. Something big! Never before in their lives had she or Pen or Finn been a part of something this fantastic.

"You'll have to excuse me for a moment while I check my records," Mayor Normal shouted out into the silence of the evening. "Just one moment, please." She stepped away from the stage.

Everyone looked around, wondering what was going on. "I'm sure nothing's wrong, right?" Penelope asked, squeezing her brother into a hug under her arm. "She's just making sure?"

Molly nodded, but she was a teensy bit nervous again. Suddenly, a warm, familiar arm draped across her shoulders and Molly looked up to see her mother's face smiling down at her proudly. "You did something extraordinary tonight," Bree Quirk said.

"Penelope and Finn were the real heroes," Molly said. "I just helped them come up with the ideas."

"No," Bree said softly. "You also made them believe it was possible. That takes a special kind of power."

Molly smiled, because she knew that was true. "Mum?" Molly said quietly.

"Yes, dear heart?" Her mother leaned in close.

"You know I didn't mean it when I said I hate being a Quirk, right?" Molly nuzzled into her mother's wild hair and hugged her close. "I really do love being a part of our family. And the thing is, well, life would be pretty boring if we were just like everyone else." She looked up at her mother and smiled. "I think we can probably figure out a way to fit in, just as we are."

Bree Quirk looked her daughter in the eye

and smiled. "You're a special girl, Molly Quirk.
We're lucky you're one
of us."

As Finn and Penel-
ope crushed into their
hug, Mayor Normal
stepped back up onstage
again. She tapped the
microphone, then began
to speak. "I'm afraid I
have some bad news,"
she said. The entire
town of Normal released
a collective groan. "Sadly,
it was close. Too close. In
fact," the mayor said, "if
we'd had just one more
piece of gum to stick to the
top of the ball, we would
have reached our goal. But
we're totally out of gum –
and it's only three minutes
before ten, so I'm afraid our fate is sealed."

Everyone began speaking at once. "Check your purses for spare gum!" someone cried.

"Just one more gumball," a kid yelled. "Come on!"

But after a lot of shuffling and even more head-shaking, no more gum was found. It was absolute chaos as everyone let it sink in: they had failed.

"One piece short?" Penelope muttered. "One piece?!"

"Hey," Molly said, trying to comfort her. "If it hadn't been for you, we would have been hundreds of pieces short."

"Close only counts in bumper bowling," Finn grumbled. "And farts."

Penelope and Bree pulled him close, trying to cheer him up. Grandpa joined them and ruffled Finn's hair. They were all disappointed that Normal hadn't succeeded, but Finn looked absolutely heartbroken.

That's when Molly realised something. They could see him – which meant one very important thing: Finn was still chewing a piece of gum! She remembered him taking one of the last gumballs from the machine when he was filling it.

Then he'd popped it into his mouth so he wouldn't go see-through again. And now, it was *still* in his mouth.

"Finn!" she whispered sharply, standing inside the circle of her family. "You're still chewing a piece of gum!"

"I know," he said, hanging his head.

Molly reached her fingers under his chin and tilted his face up so he was looking at her. She looked to Penelope, then back again. "You need to spit it out – if you add your piece to the pile, we'll break the record!"

Finn shook his head. "But I can't," he said quietly, pointing at the crowds of people that sur-rounded them. "If I take it out of my mouth, everyone will see me disappear. I'll fade away, right in front of everyone. We'll beat the record, but the Quirks will be done done done in Normal. And I don't want to leave."

"Maybe we won't have to," Penelope whispered. They all turned to look at her. "Maybe I can help."

Molly grinned. "Do you think you can do it,

Pen?" She chewed her lip. "When Finn takes the gum out of his mouth, do you think you can make him stay visible?"

"I can try," Penelope said with a nod.

Both Molly and Finn stared at their sister, wondering. They were all thinking the same thing: What if it didn't work? Would Finn fade, right in the centre of Normal, with everyone watching?

Molly twisted at the curl behind her ear while she gazed around at the crowd of friends that surrounded them. Finn chomped at his gum nervously. Penelope tried to look confident, but Molly could sense her sister's fear. They all knew that if it didn't work, the family would be heading to Texas first thing in the morning. But if it did . . .

Molly was sure it was worth the risk. She was sure her sister could do it. Finally, she nodded back.

Penelope closed her eyes. "I want this to work, more than anything. Go, Finn. Quick, before it's too late!"

Finn ran to the centre of the square, while his sisters watched and waited. He dashed up to the golden platter and shouted, "Miss Mayor! I've got one last piece! The winning piece of gum is right here, in my mouth." He opened his jaw up as wide as it would go and shouted, "Look back there at my molars!"

Mayor Normal grinned, then she pointed to the ball of ABC gum. "Go ahead, young man."

Finn strode proudly forward and reached his hand into his mouth. The whole town stared at him, completely still and totally silent. Finn looked back at Molly and Penelope once, then lifted the gum out of his mouth. Molly closed her eyes – she couldn't watch. She just held her sister's hand tightly beside her, and wished and wished for it to work.

Suddenly, everyone around them gasped. Molly couldn't stop her eyes from flying open.

Finn's fingers were outstretched, and he'd just placed the final piece on to the giant, sticky ball of gum. It stuck up like a tiny mountain on the top of the gooey ball. Cheers erupted from all around them. Finn was pumping his fist in the air. Molly looked at Penelope, and saw that she, too, was beaming.

"You did it," Molly gasped, realising that everyone around them could still see Finn. He was still visible . . . *and* he'd put the final, perfect piece on the giant ball of chewed-up gum.

"No," Penelope said. "*We* did it."

"You're right," Molly said. "The Quirks did it – together. And you know what?" She grinned at her sister. "Remember that bet? You owe me ten bucks. Because I think Normal might work out just fine."

* * *

"Look this way and smile!" Mayor Normal shouted into her microphone to get everyone's attention a short while later. She pointed to a photographer perched at the top of a giant ladder. "We did it, friends! Let's get a picture for the paper!"

The whole town squeezed in close. The Quirk kids stood at the centre of the crowd, in front of the world's largest ball of ABC gum. It was a sticky mess that they had helped build, and Molly was sure she had never seen anything so beautiful in her entire life.

As the people of their community wrapped around the Quirks, folding them into the middle,

Molly felt happy. She glanced over to smile at her mum, who was laughing with Mr Intihar – she looked relaxed, Molly thought, for the first time in a long time. Charlie and Finn – who was still fully visible, thanks to Pen – kept yelling knock-knock jokes to each other from either side of the ball of gum. Grandpa Quill was dancing a silly jig with a couple of other guys from the band. And Penelope was busy chatting with Stella and Izzy, who'd come over to stand beside them for the picture. As she watched her family fitting in, Molly felt a rush of pride and belonging, and her smile almost split her face in two.

"On three!" the photographer shouted.

"One . . ." Molly and Penelope both wrapped an arm around their brother, then smiled at the camera.

"Two . . ." Finn stuck his tongue out and wiggled it.

"Three!"

Just as the flash exploded in a burst of light, Penelope gasped and looked down. "Uh-oh," she said, turning to Molly. "Finn's disappeared again."

EPILOGUE

And Then . . .

There was one lone grump in Normal, Michigan, who skipped Normal Night and instead watched reports of her town's most ridiculous celebration on the news. Witnessing the mayhem and the mess of gum and the shrieking kids on TV was enough for her. She'd developed an acute allergy to children, and the town's festival would have made her itchy, that was for sure.

Frankly, Mrs DeVille was glad she'd stayed at home.

But now she'd grown tired of the news. The only interesting thing she'd learned all night was that the strange neighbour boy had turned into some sort of town hero. The TV people had shortened the weather report to broadcast more of the festival, which really irked her. She needed to know if she should put on her warm jumper or her very warm jumper when she woke up.

"I don't like the look of those Quirks," she muttered, flicking off the TV. "There's just something about them." She didn't like the strange sounds she heard coming from her neighbours' house when no one was supposed to be at home, and she was sure she'd seen something large and hairless and lumpy sitting on the family's back deck. Mrs DeVille vowed to keep a closer eye on her neighbours, starting immediately.

She peered outside from behind her curtains, pulling them tight around her face. Only her glasses and the wide, flat bridge of her nose were showing. Mrs DeVille stared out into the dark night, watching as some sort of bird fluttered down on to the Quirks' front porch. She hated birds. They left droppings on her steps and chirped too loudly for her taste. This bird had been hiding inside the stinking willow tree that made a mess of her neighbours' front garden. "That's like no bird I've ever seen," Mrs DeVille announced, pressing her glasses up on her nose. Her eyes bulged. "That bird looks more like a woman. What in the . . . what?" She let her curtains fall closed.

Mrs DeVille had seen a few things in her days, but this was something else altogether. Something fishy was going on over at her neighbours' place, and she was going to find out what they were hiding. She didn't like secrets, and she didn't like not knowing things she needed to know. She rubbed at her weary calves, which were squeezed inside a pair of nubby nylons, then stood up with a groan. Mrs DeVille opened her door and crept out to the front stoop for a better look. Whatever it was that had been fluttering around next door was gone now.

She looked over at the Quirks' house, and listened to the sounds of the celebration still coming from the town centre. No one was around. She was the only person at home on the whole block, and all she wanted was a little peek. It was her duty to keep an eye on the comings and goings in the neighbour-hood, wasn't it?

That's when Mrs DeV-ille got an idea.

She hobbled down her front walk and clumsily tiptoed past the Quirks' oddly pink fence. She took a deep breath and climbed up the crumbling steps.

Mrs DeVille didn't notice the tiny fairy grand-mother who flitted past her, and couldn't hear when Gran gasped. Mrs DeVille leaned against the rail on the Quirks' front porch, moving faster than

she knew she could, when it creaked under the weight of her heavy backside.

Moments later, as she stood hidden from view by a fake potted plant, Mrs DeVille peered through the tiny window in the Quirks' front door. What she saw sitting on the couch nearly gave her a heart attack. "What in tarnation is going on in there?"

FIND OUT HOW THE QUIRKS HANDLE GRUMPY MRS DEVILLE. DON'T MISS

The Quirks in Circus Quirkus!

Acknowlededgments

I have had so much support from friends and family while creating *The Quirks* that it would be impossible to thank everyone individually. But there are a few people who played an especially big role in bringing this book to life:

First, thanks to my early readers: Beth Dunfey, Maria Barbo, Robin Wasserman, Kurt Soderberg, Greg Downing, Milla Downing (and Henry and Ruby Downing, who listened intently as I read aloud). I would be a melty mess without my writing buddies and day-to-day cheerleaders: Catherine Clark, Robin (again), Kelly Barnhill. I am also happy to have found a supportive children's literature community in Minneapolis, a group of creative geniuses who always make me laugh at our monthly get-togethers – thank you.

I am in awe of Kelly Light's beautiful illustrations that brought my imagination to life.

The students and teachers at Burroughs Elementary School inspired many ideas and names that pop up in this story.

I really won the lottery with my publishing team. My agent, Michael Bourret, is amazing and an always-calming force. Michelle Nagler, my brilliant editor, has stood beside me for many years as both a great friend and story fixer. And a heartfelt thanks to the rest of the team at Bloomsbury – especially Brett Wright, Cindy Loh, Melissa Kavonic, Patricia McHugh, Regina Castillo, Ronnie Ambrose, Donna Mark, Katy Hershberger and Beth Eller – who have believed in my quirky book from the beginning and helped to make it so much better.

Most important, thanks to my family, who are my everything. Hugs for my parents, Kurt and Barb Soderberg, who showed me how a family can fit together. Cheers to my welcoming parents-in-law, Steve and Peggy Downing. Thanks to my hilarious and quirky kids, Milla, Henry and Ruby, who make me laugh (and who make up naughty stories about what our family's imaginary fourth child is doing). Finally, *thank you* to my husband, Greg, who gives me the time to write and reads everything a hundred times – I love you.